Wes
Bla   Blair,
       Trouble

D1532324

DATE	ISSUED TO	
OCT 20 '98	JAN 30	AUG 1 9 2004
MAR 25 '99	MAR 06	FEB 2 1 2008
FEB 05	JUL 1 5 2003	DEC 1 2 2008
FEB 09		APR 1 7 2009
		APR 2 4 2012
JUL 1 5 2000		JUL 0 6 2012

Wes ⊕
  Bla   Blair, Clifford
         Trouble town

Trouble Town

TROUBLE TOWN

□

CLIFFORD BLAIR

AVALON BOOKS
THOMAS BOUREGY AND COMPANY, INC.
401 LAFAYETTE STREET
NEW YORK, NEW YORK 10003

PRINTED IN THE UNITED STATES OF AMERICA
ON ACID-FREE PAPER
BY HADDON CRAFTSMEN, SCRANTON, PENNSYLVANIA

With love to Linda, my big sister, who was there when I needed her while I was growing up.

Prologue

The sentry had concealed himself atop the cliff at the entrance to the canyon where the rustlers were holed up. Winchester in hand, he crouched and watched the terrain below him with the wary eyes of a hunted man.

Clint Bradlock had spent an hour getting into position behind the sentry. His approach had taken him on foot up a rugged stone hill and across a jagged plain of rock. It had not been easy. The Wichita Mountains, here in the southwestern part of Oklahoma Territory, had long been a haven for hunted human scavengers. The tortuous landscape of hidden ravines, blind draws, and sparse vegetation made the range of low mountains ideal for eluding pursuit and hiding out. Clint knew all too well the dangers of a manhunt in this region. He had done it before.

His quarry and their booty of a dozen high-blooded horses had finally gone to ground in an easily defensible canyon. He guessed that the other two rustlers were busy changing the brands on the horses. The trio would

1

then be able to leisurely haze the animals northward to Kansas for eventual sale.

Their work at altering the brands was almost done, Clint calculated, which meant that his own time was growing short. He did not want to risk their leaving the canyon once they were finished. The canyon made a good stronghold for them, but it could also make a good trap.

Clint had trailed the trio from the site of their raid, the Double H Ranch outside the territorial capital of Guthrie. This was not the first time the Double H holdings had been hit of late. Clint had already visited the area in his ceaseless vigilance over the widespread interests of his remote employers. It had been easy for him to pick up the trail shortly after the rustlers' raid had been discovered. He doubted that the trio knew of his presence on their trail, but they were obviously pros and taking no chances.

The early autumn sun was hot on Clint where he lay in concealment. His saddle gun was beside him; his .45 was holstered at his waist. His worn trail clothes were virtually colorless. He knew they blended with the ocher shadings of the terrain, as did the high Apache moccasins he wore.

He watched the guard with growing impatience, mentally berating the man's alertness. These rustlers were not your common cow town variety of outlaws, he reminded himself again. The guard had the look of a fighting man about him—from his Winchester to his competently slung Colt and his wary, predatory air.

He was not going to be an easy victim. He might not be a victim at all.

Clint slid his right hand down along his side and withdrew the heavy bowie knife from its leather sheath. He had darkened the massive blade by fire to prevent it from casting a betraying gleam. His fingers settled comfortably into the grooves that had been fashioned in the hilt to match his grip.

He did not want to kill the guard. He never killed if he could avoid it, but there were far too many times when he could not. He hoped this wouldn't be one of them.

A low-flying buzzard skimmed past the guard's position, its notched black wings widespread as it rode a downdraft of the breeze. The guard's head turned to follow the giant bird's flight. Clint offered a silent prayer of thanks. Then he rose up from the ground to take his victim.

At the last moment, maybe sensing the swift movement of air, the guard started to turn. The hilt of Clint's bowie hammered twice against his temple in a second's time. His legs buckled. Clint caught his Winchester deftly as it fell from spasmed hands.

Swiftly Clint knelt to bind his victim. Here was one less lost soul to haunt his conscience. He retrieved the Winchester and left the sentry behind him as he moved on into the canyon. From ahead, he heard a horse's shrill whinny shift into a cry of pain. He thought he detected the stench of burned hair and flesh. Good. The other two rustlers would still be intent on their work. If they were professionals of the same caliber as their sentry, he would need every edge he could get.

The canyon became a natural stone-walled arena where scattered clumps of grass had managed to take root. Clint crouched behind a low ridge and studied the layout. The dozen stolen horses were tethered in a picket line. They seemed to be in good shape, but Clint saw tossing heads, trembling muscles, and rolling eyes. The animals were nervous, terrified of their strange surroundings and the inexplicable torture that some of them had already undergone.

The two rustlers were just releasing their latest horse. They had obviously taken the animal from the picket line and tied it by a lead rope to a convenient wiry blackjack oak. One of them had then lassoed its hind legs and stretched it out so that the altering brand could be applied. It was as good a method as any, and a fire burned nearby for the branding iron. Clint wondered how they were changing the Double H brand.

The horse—a sorrel mare—scrambled to its feet as its hind legs were freed. It shook itself and sidestepped a little as if to escape the pain that must be biting at its seared hip. Clint spotted the rustlers' horses tethered nearby. The pair's saddle guns were in their sheaths. Each of them carried a handgun, and one of them had some kind of a fighting knife.

They looked to be pros too, Clint thought, although at the moment they were placing a little too much faith in their sentry. Men of this hard breed were being pressured more and more by the encroachment of civilization across what had once been the lawless lands assigned to the remnants of various Indian tribes. Clint knew a perverse sort of empathy for the rustlers; he felt the same pressure himself. But the plundering and murders of such outlaws could never be justified or tolerated.

The so-called Unassigned Lands had been opened just a few years earlier by the famous Land Run of 1889, and the steady flow of homesteaders and settlers into the area had resulted in the openings of additional Indian lands to the east. In a few short years the Cheyennes, the Arapahos, the Cherokees, the Comanches, and other tribes had been forced inexorably from the lands that had recently been promised to them forever.

There had been other land runs during some of these openings, but none to compare with the chaotic rush of '89, when sixty thousand people on horses and in vehicles ranging from prairie schooners to bicycles had raced and fought one another for the choice pieces of land. Of course, many of those pieces had already been claimed by the Sooners, settlers who had made illegal early entries into the lands. If need be, they would defend them with lead and blood from the legitimate settlers.

That wild, violent rush of humanity was a symbol of sorts for the spread of the homesteaders across this rolling plains country, Clint mused. During that period, his enigmatic employers had moved shrewdly to amass their great holdings in the dynamic new territory. Statehood was not far off, and their acquisitions would allow them to take advantage of the inevitable economic boom. Their enterprise had also given Clint his job of watchdog, protector, and, sometimes, vigilante for their holdings.

The owlhoots and long riders had long considered these lands their own, a refuge from the scattered and overworked lawmen responsible for the area. Now, with homesteaders moving into what had once been open range, the scavengers found themselves faced with easier targets offset by increased pressure from lawmen. They reacted with characteristic violence, and a state of near-open warfare existed between the out-laws and the settlers. The long riders were doomed to lose in the long run, Clint knew, but in the interim, blood would be shed and lives would be lost—perhaps his own, too, if he wasn't careful with this current pair.

The one who had worked the horses was preparing to release the mare from the makeshift snubbing post. His companion shoved the branding iron back into the fire. Sparks exploded. Clint levered his Winchester softly.

"End of the trail, boys," he called out. "Stand where you are!"

They froze.

"Dead drop," Clint told them. "Shuck your belts."

Almost imperceptibly the horse handler edged his head around to see his companion. The brand wielder gave the slightest of nods. Clint could tell from the easing of their muscles that the decision had been made to comply with his command. Pros. Only greenhorns went up against an unseen enemy with a clear shot. Both gun belts dropped.

"Kick them away."

They obeyed with little enthusiasm. The guns were still close, but Clint had expected nothing better.

Now came the touchy part. Clint straightened and stepped out into the open. His Winchester was leveled. These two would never be completely harmless until they had coins placed over their dead eyes.

"Hands up. Higher. Turn your backs to me."

He moved closer. Both of them were straining to get a look at him over their shoulders. He didn't object. Let them see the rifle. It might stifle any thoughts they had of jumping him. He could have ordered one of them to tie the other, but he couldn't have trusted the results. He needed one of them immobilized so that he could handle them separately.

He moved swiftly forward and brought the butt of his Winchester around in a short, sharp arc. They had been expecting it, and the horseman ducked away from the stroke. It caught him glancingly and stumbled him forward. Peripherally, Clint saw the other one turn and stoop for his discarded gun belt. Clint swiveled toward him. The owlhoot had his handgun free and was swinging back around. Clint fired, levered the Winchester, and fired again. The rustler went backward on collapsing legs.

Booted feet scuffled the ground behind Clint. He spun toward the sound. The horseman had his fighting knife out. It had not been on his gun belt, Clint realized.

He was good with it. It arced in a savage slash at Clint's midriff. The outlaw almost ran into the barrel of the swinging Winchester as Clint brought it around. Clint shot him in the middle. His closeness muffled the shot, which doubled him convulsively. He toppled off to the side as Clint stepped back and levered the Winchester again.

There was no need. Both of them were down. The horseman was gut-shot and dying, and his partner, Clint recognized at a glance, was dead. Slowly Clint straightened out of his instinctive crouch. The horses were snorting and shying skittishly. They didn't like the smell of death any better than he did. He tried to ignore the fact that his legs were trembling. The pair had made their own choice, but a bitterness shriveled his mouth. *Two more lost souls,* he thought. His employers' holdings carried a higher and higher price.

He sighed and began to examine the horses. They were in good-enough shape and would make the trip back all right. He looked at the bodies. First he would have to bury them and say a few futile words over the graves. He thought of the bound sentry back at the mouth of the canyon. It was going to be a long trek back to Guthrie with a string of horses and a dangerous prisoner in tow.

Chapter One

The hooves of Clint's paint stallion clattered on the bricks that paved Guthrie's major streets. The sounds were all but lost in the familiar clamor of life in the territorial capital. Wagons and buggies vied for room with horsemen and hurrying pedestrians. Clint's flicking eyes took in busy townspeople, impassive Indians, lounging cowhands. The varied scents of bustling humanity and thriving enterprise rode the air currents.

Guthrie had been birthed overnight as a tent city following the wild Land Run of '89. In the few years since then, it had matured into a lusty metropolis with running water, electric lights, and a system of tunnels connecting many of its business establishments. Saloons, banks, hotels, and stores crowded the main streets. Elaborate turrets and pressed tin moldings adorned many buildings. The architecture combined the elegance of a Victorian city with the untamed spirit of the West.

Clint reined in at a public watering trough. He dismounted and let the paint drink sparingly. Then he worked the handle of the pump until a fresh stream of cold well water cascaded out. Doffing his Stetson, he drank long and deep from it. He savored its pure taste and its coolness on his face. Dripping, he let the paint drink again.

He had left the horses at the Double H spread outside of town. A message had been awaiting him there. He had lingered long enough to clean the trail dust from himself. Reaching Guthrie, he had dropped his sullen prisoner off at the office of U.S. Deputy Marshal Heck Thomas. He recounted the story of the man's capture to the tough, aging lawman and saw the prisoner locked safely away in the grim cell block. Thomas promised to check for outstanding bounties.

His thirst now slaked, Clint tied the paint at the hitching rail, where it settled into a patient hipshot stance. Clint pulled out his railroad watch. The message for him at the ranch had advised him of a meeting in town. With his customary and uncanny intuition, Thom Chancery had been able to pinpoint almost to the hour when he would return with the stolen horses and be available for a meeting, Clint mused. He wondered sometimes just how Chancery managed to do it.

He still had a few minutes to spare, and he maneuvered his way across the crowded street to the Blue Belle Saloon. The notorious bar was adjacent to the hotel where Chancery had scheduled their meeting. He pushed into the saloon and sidestepped a little to take his unguarded back out of the doorway. He paused as he roamed his eyes over the room. It was not large. A scattering of tables occupied the floor in front of the bar. A table of poker players barely noted his entrance. A couple of cowhands were at another table with a half empty bottle of whiskey between them. They glanced at him with little interest. Then one of them reached for the bottle.

A saloon girl watched him with wary hunger from the bar. Heavy makeup did an inadequate job of covering the bruises on her face. *Rough night*, Clint thought. A frail kid with a Colt too big for him eyed Clint with a different kind of hunger. Like instinctively recognizes like, Clint thought with an edge of pain. He almost turned and left, because he wasn't in the mood for trouble of that sort. Instead, he went on into the bar. Backing away from such trouble wasn't part of his character or his hard-won reputation.

As Stan, the barkeep, gave him a troubled look, Clint knew that he had read the situation right. ''A beer,'' he said.

Stan nodded. He glanced unhappily at the kid, then turned to fill the order. Clint accepted the mug left-handed. Conscious of the kid's eyes gauging him, he shifted toward a nearby table, careful not to turn his back fully to the kid.

He sat down and held his beer without sipping it. He rarely drank; alcohol slowed the reflexes and dulled the mind. Drinking was plain stupidity for a man who made his living by his guns and his wits.

He avoided glancing at the kid. They all seemed to

look the same to him by now. Their faces and their guns might be different, but the latent violence in their eyes was always the same. *How old is this one?* he wondered. *Seventeen? Eighteen? Not much more than a child.* The thought gave him a chill.

"I ain't seen you around here before." The kid's voice was deep—almost a man's voice.

"Count your blessings." Clint didn't look up. His peripheral vision was alert for movement.

"Forget it, son," Stan advised from behind the bar.

"I ain't your son!"

Stan fell silent. Clint sat very still.

"You're wearing a gun and a knife like you're a fighting man." The kid stepped clear of the bar.

Clint looked around at him for the first time. "That's something you don't want to find out," he said evenly. *Slap a gun on the wrong kind of kid and he stops being a kid and becomes a potential killer*, Clint thought. *He becomes so eager for the nebulous glory of a gunman's rep that he'll pick a fight with any prospect that comes along.*

"That's Clint Bradlock, son," Stan interjected. "You don't want to pull on him."

"Bradlock?" The kid was staring now. "You don't look man enough to be Bradlock, not with the rep he carries."

"I'm old enough to be the death of you," Clint said. "Without even standing up."

"You're really Bradlock?" Awe had touched his voice.

Clint nodded at the holstered Colt. "You got one sure way of finding out."

The kid hesitated. Fear emerged to tinge the feral eagerness and the sudden respect on his face.

Clint didn't want to kill him. "It ain't worth it," he told him. "You're looking to make a name for yourself. The only way you'll do it here is as one more notch on my reputation."

The kid wavered. Clint watched as the will to fight died within him. A stricken look came over his face, making him seem even more youthful. His eyes darted to the room's other occupants. Clint realized that their encounter had become the center of attention. The muscles in the kid's face twisted. Wordlessly, he turned and all but bolted from the bar.

Stan heaved a sigh of relief. When one of the poker players started to laugh, Clint swung his head sharply toward him. The laughter died abruptly. Clint rose from the table. His beer was untouched. He was aware of the bar girl's longing stare. At least the kid was alive, he told himself. There were worse things than facing life after having your nerve broken. There had to be. The kid would live longer now. Clint looked down at his beer. He almost drank, but he knew it wouldn't quench his thirst.

He sidestepped from behind the table and left the saloon. No one was waiting for him outside. The kid hadn't had second thoughts about trying to take him. Clint crossed the alley to the hotel, where he was probably late for his appointment.

Thom Chancery's suite was on the second floor. Clint knocked at the solid oak door, and after a moment Chancery himself opened it. The Western business agent for the Partners was hard and compact in face and body. Silver was beginning to slash at his dark hair. He was not tall, but he rarely gave the impression of looking up to anyone.

"Clint. Good to see you." His handshake was hard and dry. Clint had never seen Chancery sweat.

Chancery ushered him into the suite. A businessmen's boardroom, complete with polished mahogany table, was adjacent to the plush sitting room. Chancery always went high dollar, but then the Partners could certainly afford it.

"Have a seat." Effortlessly, Chancery whipped a heavy chair around from the table for him. "They sent a rider from the ranch. Congratulations on recovering the horses. Good job. I was hoping you'd be back in time to get my message."

"Something up?" Clint asked.

Chancery moved with natural ease to the head of the table. He did not sit down, but faced Clint from behind the chair there. In his tailored suit he might have been a ruthless bank president presiding over a board meeting. "We've got trouble."

"The Good Book says there's nothing new under the sun," Clint said drily.

Chancery moved his firm lips from side to side as if he were chewing. It was his one nervous mannerism.

"You know that there have been other Double H holdings that have been hit by outlaws of late."

Clint nodded.

"The owner is worried."

"Howard Herns," Clint supplied.

Chancery actually blinked. "You know who he is?"

Clint leaned back in his chair and savored Chancery's discomfiture. "You don't really think I'd work for the Partners as long as I have without knowing something about them, do you?"

Chancery worked his lips back and forth. "I had no idea."

The Partners, Clint reflected. They were an unofficial and secretive cartel of powerful Eastern businessmen who controlled or held wide interests in the Territory. From their bastions of power in the Eastern cities, they wielded subtle and powerful influence throughout the area.

"They're very pleased with your work, you know." Chancery appeared to rally from his bemusement. "Your abilities and reputation have proven invaluable in safeguarding their interests and recovering their property when occasion demands."

His carefully cultivated reputation was as important to his job as his skills with gun and knife, Clint thought. He had been willing to kill in the saloon just now in order to preserve it. His ties to the Partners were painstakingly concealed. He was known throughout the Territory as a hired gun and bounty hunter. As such, when it was necessary, he could easily gain access to men

and places when an official officer of the law would
have been met automatically with hostility and violence. He had capitalized on that reputation more than
once in his work for the Partners. *Has my reputation
grown to become the most important thing in my life?*
he now wondered with a chill that touched his spirit.

"So, Herns is worried," he said aloud to dispel the
unpleasant thought.

"He's here now."

Clint lifted his head sharply. In all his jobs for the
Partners, he had never met one of them personally.
Chancery had been his sole contact with the shadowy
group.

"He wants to meet you," Chancery went on.

Clint started to respond, then stopped. He recalled
his earlier thoughts about the Double H holdings when
he had been on the trail of the horse thieves. "Someone's working him over," he concluded aloud.

Chancery nodded. "It appears that way. Not only
the Double H but his other holdings as well have suf-
fered from what almost seems to be a systematic pattern
of plunder." Chancery paused. "But that's not our
most immediate concern, except, perhaps, that a single
piece is a part of the whole."

"What piece is that?"

"I think I'll let Mr. Herns explain further." He
raised his voice to be heard outside the conference
room: "Sir?"

Herns had apparently been waiting, because he appeared almost immediately in the doorway. Clint saw

a large, sleek man in a tailored suit that was even finer than Chancery's. Herns carried too much weight. His receding hair was slicked back, and his fleshy features seemed compressed, as if he were constantly on the verge of frowning. His eyes were shrewd as they appraised Clint.

"I'm Howard Herns." He offered a large hand as Clint rose. He met the gunman's gaze as they shook hands.

Clint found himself liking the man without quite knowing why. Perhaps it was the fact that Herns addressed him as an equal and not as a hired hand.

"I understand you've just recovered some of my stock," Herns told him once they were all seated.

Clint nodded. "Things worked out well for me."

"Nonsense. You made them work out. You have a talent for doing that, as I understand."

Clint waited.

"Something else of mine has been taken," Herns went on. "Something a lot more valuable than those horses. I need your help in recovering it."

"What is it?" Clint prodded.

Herns didn't answer directly. "I have a great many holdings in the Territory besides the Double H Ranch," he said.

Clint nodded. "I know."

Herns gave Chancery a sharp glance. He returned his attention to Clint. "You probably also know that I've been having some problems here in the Territory with outlaws and long riders."

"Any idea why they seem to be concentrating on you?" Clint asked.

Herns's features compressed even further until he was actually frowning. "Luck of the draw," he said savagely. "I don't know. It's not even common knowledge that I own assets here in the Territory." With an apparent effort he forced his face to relax somewhat. "I've been seeking to increase my holdings in this area," he explained. "I had negotiated a closing transaction and planned a trip out here to conclude it. When this trouble started, I decided to extend my stay and look things over firsthand. I've got my own private rail car and engine, so it was no major inconvenience. As it turned out, I didn't even get to finish the closing."

"What happened?"

Herns's evident anger and frustration appeared to be making it hard for him to get his story told. "The closing was for the purchase of a bank in Oklahoma City. I'm buying it from the original founders. They insisted on payment in gold—all one hundred thousand dollars of it."

"The gold was taken," Clint surmised.

Herns nodded darkly. "I had a private courier company transporting it here. Their agents were held up and robbed outside of Oklahoma City."

"And the robbers got away clean," Clint guessed.

"Two of them got away dead," Herns said with grim satisfaction. "The courier's agents aren't paid to let shipments be taken from them without a good fight. They killed two of the holdup men and pursued the third, who actually had the gold. They finally gave up the chase, however.''

''Why?''

Herns studied him closely. ''Are you familiar with White City?'' he asked.

''You mean Beer City?'' Clint's lips curled in disgust.

Herns nodded. ''That's what some call it hereabouts, I understand.''

''It's a pagan hellhole up in the Panhandle country,'' Clint said. ''Mostly just a collection of saloons and gambling houses. There's no organized law to speak of, and the citizens, if you want to call them that, are scavengers of the worst kind—gunmen, wanted men, gamblers, and prostitutes.''

''Look at this,'' Chancery said as he slid a folded newspaper down the table to Clint.

It was one of the large Eastern dailies and was folded to a quarter-page advertisement. '' 'Come to White City,' '' Clint read aloud, '' 'the only town of its kind in the civilized world, where there is absolutely no law.' '' Smaller print listed various sordid attractions, among them beer, whiskey, women, and games of chance.

''The town merchants, such as they are, have run ads like that all over the country.'' Chancery growled. ''And they're darn near right. The town is just south of the Kansas border in the Public Land Strip where there's some question as to which government, if any, has authority. The businesses there cater to the cow-

boys from the trail herds that come to Liberal and
Tyrone up in Kansas. They have strict prohibition of
liquor in that state, but it doesn't matter, because all
the trail hands have to do is to cross over the border
to White City, where they can indulge in all the vices
they can imagine. The place has also been attracting
business from all over the country with these filthy ads.
It's become quite a boomtown in its own perverse
way.''

"Is that where the third holdup man went with the
gold?'' Clint asked.

Herns nodded. ''Exactly. The courier agents refused
to follow him there.''

Clint understood why. In White City, revelation of
the agents' identities by their quarry would have been
their death warrant. The barbaric inhabitants of White
City had little love for representatives of law and order.

"We need you to go in there after the third holdup
man. With your reputation, you can safely blend in
with the locals. We think the robber is still there with
the gold. He probably feels safe,'' Herns went on.

"With reason,'' Clint murmured.

"If he's not there, try to pick up his trail and recover
the gold. Bring him in too, if you can.''

"You'll be on your own like never before,'' Chancery interjected. ''Mr. Herns and I plan to stay in the
area for the time being while he inspects his other
holdings. I've taken the calculated risk of advising
Heck Thomas, the marshal here, that you have a tem-

porary and quasi-official status as an investigator for Eastern interests. He'll be available in a pinch.''

Clint's eyes narrowed. ''White City is a long way from here,'' he commented. ''As good as he is, Heck Thomas won't be of any help there.'' He caught Chancery's gaze. ''Up till now, he's thought I'm nothing more than a bounty hunter. Next time, get my approval before you go name-dropping when it's my neck in the noose.''

Chancery's mouth worked from side to side. He nodded silent acquiescence.

''There'll be a bonus for you in addition to your usual wages,'' Herns stepped in smoothly.

Clint nodded. He was well paid by the Partners for his hazardous work. ''Make it a big one,'' he suggested.

He didn't like the sound of this mission. There were too many unknowns, from the dangers of White City to the identity of the third robber and to the possible existence of an organized pattern of plundering Herns's holdings. He wondered if the risk was worth his prospective bonus. White City sounded like a dozen kinds of trouble.

Chapter Two

Clint rode into White City. The nameless main street ran east and west, and it was lined with ramshackle bars and tawdry gaming houses. Some of the sleazy businesses even operated out of foul tents. Clint's nostrils contracted at a stench comprised of rotting trash, raw sewage, unwashed humanity, and unbridled decadence.

There was no church in White City, no school, no post office. Almost every business sold alcohol, and hence the town's nickname of Beer City. Clint could see shacks and lean-tos along some of the rutted tracks extending north and south from the main street. He spotted a single store, and it, too, doubled as a bar.

Human predators of both sexes prowled the street or watched for prey. Clint saw lounging gamblers, hard-eyed gunmen, and painted women whose eyes were just as hard as those of the gunmen. In their own way, the women had looked on as much death as any of the outlaws. They saw it every day in the eyes of their customers.

The predators regarded him with caution or with hunger. Most looked away quickly. Plainly, they recognized him as one of their own, and Clint felt an edge of sickness in his gut.

A few cowhands lounged in doorways or sprawled awkwardly in alleys. Most were not yet recovered from last night's activities. It was late afternoon and too early for the evening revelry to have begun. Clint had planned his arrival for this hour.

He rode the length of the town at a walk. Within a prizefighting ring, a heavy-muscled fighter sparred with the air. His movements were smooth and fast.

The town straggled to a halt at the end of the street. Beyond was the empty rolling grassland of the Panhandle. Clint turned his paint and retraced his route to the first of the saloons. He had already gotten a feel for this dissolute town, and he didn't like it.

Was his quarry one of the men he had passed on the street? It was entirely possible. The holdup men had been masked, and the courier agents had been unable to give a description of the one who had escaped with the gold. Was he maybe sleeping off the night's debauchery above the saloon? Was he even in town at all?

Clint had no detailed plan of action, but he had pondered the situation at length on his ride up here from Guthrie. If the robbery of the agents had been a part of some organized campaign against Herns, then it made sense to figure that White City, where the surviving robber had sought sanctuary, might somehow be the center of the campaign. And if there were such a campaign, then the death of the other robbers and his capture of the horse thieves had reduced the campaign's manpower. Whoever was recruiting pros like the horse thieves might be looking for new recruits, and a man of Clint Bradlock's reputation should be a valuable addition to the crew.

It was all guesswork and hunch, but he had little more than that to go on. Once he was a part of the organization—assuming that there actually was an organization—he might be able to find out something about the gold. But the plan was risky and he could not afford to have his true purposes become known. He grinned a little bitterly as he dismounted in front of the first saloon. Even a worm knows better than to help thread itself onto the hook, but that was exactly what he was doing.

Sawdust floor, sagging bar, rickety tables, a dim atmosphere heavy with the scents of old tobacco and stale whiskey—the first saloon had little to recommend it. But there were patrons. Clint bought a beer and took a shadowy corner table. He fended off the advances of a gaunt bar girl and a consumptive cardsharp.

He sat and listened to the murmur of conversation. After a few minutes a furtive and shifty-eyed man entered the saloon. He looked about until his gaze lighted on Clint in the dim corner. Then he looked quickly away and went to the bar. The barkeep served him, but no money changed hands. The fellow did not look in Clint's direction again.

Clint waited a while longer. Then he rose to his feet, left his unfinished beer, and went out of the saloon. The next bar along the dirt street was little better. Once more he sat and listened and watched. The shifty-eyed man entered shortly after him. He continued to ignore Clint.

After the first two, the bars and saloons and gaming houses began to blur together in Clint's mind. His furtive shadow stayed with him faithfully. Clint brushed off bar girls and grafters and limited himself to a few sips of beer at each place. As the afternoon lengthened into early evening, cowhands and farmers and family men from other towns began to drift into White City. The bar girls stopped concentrating on Clint and sought easier prey. Voices were raised in drunken laughter. Discordant music began to issue from some of the establishments. Occasional flurries of gunshots sounded. White City was stirring into dissolute life.

Clint nursed his beers and listened. He began to hear a name repeated in varying contexts and varying tones. Sometimes it was mentioned in anger, but more often in respect or even fear. Clint noted the name: Carter Brandon.

''Blast Brandon's soul!'' he heard a grizzled oldster mutter drunkenly to himself at a nearby table. ''Done had my partner killed, that's what he did. Old Zeke wasn't hurting nothing. Just blowing and going a little. Shot off a few rounds was all he did. Nobody in that danged saloon would've been hurt. Old Zeke was a better shot drunk than any of them sober. A man's got a right to carry on a little after being up in the hills all them months. It just ain't right, Brandon having him shot down thataway. Like a dog. . . .'' His words fell away into an unintelligible mumble.

Clint glanced at him surreptitiously. The old man seemed barely conscious. A nearly empty bottle of whiskey sat on the table in front of him. He had the look of a prospector about him, from his gnarled hands to his weathered skin and ragged clothing. A huge, old revolver of indeterminate make was stuck in his belt.

''Show me all them cards!'' a man's voice shouted. Clint heard chairs pushed back hurriedly. He swung his head around.

A young cowpoke had risen from his chair at a poker table. Across from him, still seated, was a hatchet-faced man with the soft hands and pale features of a gambler. The other two participants in the game had quickly moved clear.

The gambler's expression was sardonic. ''Don't play if you can't afford to lose, cowboy,'' he advised.

''I don't mind losing in an honest game!'' the cowhand shot back. He was swaying a little. Several empty beer mugs were on the table in front of him. He wore a big Colt in a holster at a high, awkward position.

''Watch it now.'' The gambler did not seem particularly concerned about the accusation or the implied threat in the cowboy's stance. ''We'll just call the game finished.''

''The devil we will! Hey, barkeep, you're my witness. Come here and look at this.'' The cowhand turned his head toward the bar as he spoke. With the casual speed of practice, the gambler pulled a short-barreled revolver from under his coat and shot the cowboy in the chest. Coldly, he shot him again as he fell. The shots boomed back and forth across the room. The smell of gunsmoke seared Clint's nostrils.

Still seated, the gambler glanced around. "Any other complaints?'' he inquired mildly.

There were no takers. The other two players were both edging toward the door. The gambler grinned at nothing in particular and resheathed his gun in his shoulder rig. He began to rake in all the money on the table.

The saloon door swung open and two men stepped authoritatively into the room. Clint typed them as gunmen. He was reminded of the hard professionalism of the rustlers. These two were no longer young, but the experience of survival was plain in their uncompromising features. Clint glanced at his shifty-eyed shadow. The little man was watching the pair almost fearfully.

They surveyed the room, then bracketed the gambler. He remained seated. His grin had not lost its edge of sarcasm. "The town enforcers,'' he said mockingly. "Glad to see you gentlemen are on the job tonight.''

"What happened, Rancon?'' one of the enforcers asked. He toed the body of the dead man. "Did he call one of your crooked hands?''

"He called my *honest* hand,'' Rancon corrected him

gently. "Accused me of cheating. I had to defend both my life and my honor."

The other gunman snorted. "You? Honor?" he jeered.

"That one didn't believe it." Rancon nodded absently at the corpse. "If he was alive, I venture to guess that he might have a different opinion now, or, at least, if not, he would keep his opinion to himself."

The gunman had stopped sneering.

"Mr. Brandon thinks your tally is getting a little high around here, Rancon," the other gunman said. "Three men dead, two over poker games and one over a woman. Now, Mr. Brandon won't hardly like it if you add very many more to that score. Too many killings can be bad for business. Keeps the customers away. Gives our town a bad reputation."

"Convey my sincere apologies to Mr. Brandon. Advise him that I'll try to be more careful in the future." A different, harder, edge had replaced the sarcasm in his tones.

"Yeah. We'll tell him."

Rancon grinned his private grin.

One of the gunhands turned to the barkeep. "Fred, send someone over to Harry's. See that this stiff gets buried. Maybe he'll be the only one tonight."

The barkeep nodded rapidly. As the two gunmen turned away from Rancon, one of them saw the grizzled old prospector glowering at them.

"You still here, you old buzzard?" They approached his table. "Mr. Brandon says you're to be gone by midnight. Might be a good idea to leave now. You wouldn't want to be late. You'd regret that a heap.''

''Blast Brandon to blazes!'' the old man muttered. ''I got till midnight and I'm staying until then. And maybe longer, if I take a mind to,'' he added defiantly.

''That'd be bad for your health. But you suit yourself. We'll be back come midnight to make sure you get your tail out of town on time.''

The oldster mumbled something incomprehensible. The two gunhands exchanged contemptuous looks. As they turned toward the door, one of them glanced toward Clint and then froze. The other sensed his companion's halt and followed the direction of his gaze.

Clint was vaguely conscious of Rancon watching the scene with gauging eyes and smiling his bizarre smile. Clint raised his beer mug in a salute to the gunhands. The first one nodded in acknowledgment. His companion did not react. Together they looked toward the shifty-eyed little man. Then they continued out of the saloon.

Chancery and Herns had been wrong, Clint mused. White City did have law, although it was of a primitive and violent sort. He guessed that the grizzled oldster's partner had been shot down by enforcers like this pair in order to protect White City's equivalent of innocent bystanders. Recalling the newspaper advertisement that sought to lure business to the town, he supposed that its leading vice merchants did have a vested interest in not letting things get too rowdy. Rancon, the gambler, was plainly on the edge of being declared an undesirable.

Clint rose to his feet and sauntered after the two gunmen. He thought he felt Rancon's grin directed at his back as he left the saloon. It was dark outside, but he could see the enforcers just entering another drinking establishment farther down the street.

Their relaxed attitudes indicated they were no longer on official business. They had probably been responding to the sounds of Rancon's shots when they had come to the saloon. How many more enforcers were there? Clint wondered. He followed in the pair's wake.

The saloon they had entered was one of the most prosperous-looking ones on the street. It was a wide, two-story, frame building. Over the doorway a picture of an elephant had been painted above the name Elephant Saloon. Clint studied the weathered painting as he approached. He wondered how the place had come by its odd name.

The door stood open. Clint let his hand brush over the familiar butt of his .45 before he stepped through the door. The interior of the place was also nicer than the other rat holes he had seen in this town. The Elephant Saloon boasted a wooden floor, an elaborate hardwood bar backed by a long mirror, gaming and customer tables, and even a small elevated stage. A stairway led upward at the back of the long room. Business was good, and painted women circulated among cardplayers and drinkers. A haze of smoke hung in the air, and the raw smell of alcohol cut through it like a knife.

It took Clint a moment to spot the two enforcers. They were maneuvering their way through the press toward a big man at the bar with a redheaded woman at his side.

Clint let his eyes slide away. The pair would be easy to keep track of in the saloon. He sought out an unoccupied table near the wall and seated himself. The enforcers were talking to the big man. Their stances were respectful. Clint could see little of the man to whom they seemed to be reporting.

A faded bar girl swayed up to his table, but Clint barely glanced at her. He ordered a beer. She sniffed and moved away. Women like her could be valuable sources of information, but they could also betray a man in a single wink of a mascaraed eye.

Clint noticed that the shifty-eyed fellow had also entered the saloon. Clint eyed him openly as the fellow looked about the busy room. His eyes fell on Clint, then met Clint's probing gaze. The little man looked quickly away and began to sidle toward the bar. Clint watched with interest as he drew near the two enforcers and hovered there, as if waiting for them to complete their business with their boss.

Glancing around the room, Clint spotted six other men with the tough look of professionals. Some seemed aloof from the revelry. Perhaps they were on duty. Others appeared intent only on enjoying themselves. He saw one of them ascending the stairs with a bar girl. Her smile, he was sure, went no deeper than her makeup.

He looked again at the bar. The two enforcers had finished their report and retreated. The shifty-eyed man had taken their place. He was speaking quickly. After a minute the big man moved slightly to see past him. He gazed directly at Clint. For the first time Clint could see his face clearly. It was a hard, competent face, not yet old, but weathered by experience. The brow was high, the eyes were wide-set, and the mouth was a little too thin above a square jaw that looked as though it could take a good punch without damage. The hair was thick and brown. Hatless, the big man wore range clothes with the comfortable ease of long habit.

He appeared to study Clint without expression as the little man continued to speak. Next he nodded dismissal to his underling without removing his gaze from Clint. The little man skulked away with an air of relief. His master left the bar and threaded his way through the press toward Clint. Pouting, the redhead at the bar watched him go. Clint noted a lean gunhand also begin to drift in his direction from the bar.

The big man stopped. He was close enough so that Clint had to look up slightly to see his face. He was also close enough, if need be, to kick the table over onto Clint. Clint took in his powerful build and his lean, capable hands. The man was hard and tough, with nothing showy about him except the gun holstered at his side. It was not the typical revolver favored by most Westerners. Rather, it was some sort of automatic pistol. The shells would be fed by magazine instead of by a revolving cylinder. Clint guessed it was of European make, although he could not see it clearly.

"You're a stranger here." The big man's voice was surprisingly soft.

"I'd guess you'd know, seeing as how you've had me watched since I hit town," Clint drawled.

The thin lips twitched as if their owner almost thought the remark was amusing. "What are you doing here?" he asked bluntly.

"The Good Book says, 'Seek and ye shall find,' " Clint answered. "That's what I'm doing—seeking."

"Seeking what?"

"Whatever I can find."

The thin lips grew thinner. "Who are you, cowboy?" He made the demand with the authority of a man who had the right to know.

"Name's Clint Bradlock."

His reputation again. Some of the tension eased out of the other man. "I've heard tell of you." The dark, wide-spaced eyes appraised him coldly. "Are you as good as they say you are?"

"I'm alive."

This time there was a smile and a quick, harsh bark of laughter. "And coming from someone with your rep, I guess that means something," he conceded.

"You got a name?" Clint asked insolently.

"I'm Carter Brandon."

The revelation came as no surprise. Clint waved his left hand to take in the saloon. "You own all this?"

Brandon snorted. "Not on a bet. I'll leave the ownership of this town in other hands than mine, and welcome to it. No, you might say I'm head of White City's militia and law enforcement all rolled into one. I provide security around here."

"All by yourself?"

Brandon frowned. His dark eyes turned inward. "Was the time when I rode this trouble town alone," he said without boasting. His eyes came back from the past. "But now I've got a security force. Enforcers, I call them. I expect you've noticed a few of them around."

Clint nodded. "A few."

"We keep it safe for the merchants and their customers."

Clint thought of Rancon and the dead cowboy. "I've noticed that too," he commented.

"White City is different from any other town in this country," Brandon said seriously. "If you stay here long enough, you'll appreciate what that means."

"Any reason why I shouldn't stay?" Clint inquired mildly.

"I guess that comes back to what it is you're seeking."

"What's here to find?"

Brandon considered him. "Maybe the kind of a deal a man like you is always looking for."

Behind Brandon, Clint saw a surge of movement in the crowd. Several men stepped hurriedly clear. The grizzled old prospector who had lost his partner had left the other saloon, but he had not left town. He lifted his huge old revolver and lined it shakily between Brandon's shoulder blades.

"Cover your back!" Clint yelled at Brandon.

He had his own .45 out as Brandon turned. He didn't have a clear shot. Brandon's movement was a tight, hard swivel. One swift hand leaped to take the odd automatic and sweep it level. Brandon fired three times, so fast that Clint thought it was impossible. The shots stuttered together as one. The old man danced backward on his toes. His outstretched gun arm dropped in a series of jerking movements. The big revolver was unfired. It hit the floor beside him as he fell.

"Filthy old coot!" Brandon rasped savagely as the echoes died. He pointed the pistol as if he would put another shot into the shrunken form. Then he jerked it up unfired and looked around furiously. "Buck!" he roared.

"Yes sir, Mr. Brandon." The lean gunfighter whom Clint had noticed earlier appeared from the crowd. His face was pale.

"You were supposed to be watching my back! Where the blazes were you?"

"Right here, Mr. Brandon. I couldn't help it. He was just there all of a sudden. I couldn't get a good shot. . . ." His voice trailed off at the anger edging Brandon's features.

"Your gun ain't even drawn! I ought to kill you too!" Brandon yelled viciously.

Clint had no doubt that Brandon could bring the

unholstered pistol into play again long before Buck cleared leather. Buck obviously had no doubts, either. He sucked in a deep breath and didn't let it out. His gun hand began to shake. He stammered wordlessly.

"Get out of here!" Brandon snapped. "Don't come back to White City or I'll bury you here!"

Buck's breath came out in a rush. He managed a jerky nod, turned, and hurried from the saloon. Brandon watched him go as he reholstered the pistol.

"Now get this carrion out of here." Brandon gestured at the prospector's body. Several men rushed to obey. Brandon turned back to Clint. "Thanks."

Clint's .45 was in its holster once more. He nodded acknowledgment.

"I saw you draw," Brandon went on.

"I didn't have a clear shot, either." Clint's tone was dry.

Brandon shrugged. "You weren't being paid to. He was. He's lucky I didn't kill him." Brandon stepped to the table, pulled out a chair, and seated himself. As the prospector's body was being carried out, Brandon didn't spare it a glance, and regarding Clint with his wide-spaced eyes, he said, "You and I need to talk."

Chapter Three

"We didn't get down to details last night," Brandon said. "We can go over those now. Drink?"

"No, thanks," Clint told him.

Brandon lifted an ironic eyebrow over one dark eye. "That's right. You're not much of a drinking man, are you? Noticed that last night." He turned to the barkeep behind the bar. "Whiskey," he ordered.

A lone gun hand was stationed near the end of the bar. He divided his attention between Brandon and the other saloon occupants. *The luckless Buck's replacement*, Clint figured.

Even at that hour of midmorning, the Elephant Saloon was doing a fair amount of business. From where Clint stood with his back against the mahogany bar and his elbows on the brass rail, he could survey the entire room. A couple of poker games were going on, a bar girl was helping a trio of cowhands to guzzle their rotgut, and a scattering of barflies were interested only in their bottles.

"The place never closes," Brandon remarked as if he had read Clint's thoughts. He tossed off the whiskey that the barkeep had brought him.

Clint hadn't needed to be told, because the sounds of the saloon had filtered to the small upstairs room where he had spent the night at Brandon's insistence. He hadn't had anyplace else to go, and accepting the offer made sense if he wanted to get in close with Brandon. But his sleep had been light. Only a fool slept heavily in the lion's den.

"Are you sure you don't own a piece of this?" he inquired now.

Brandon shook his head. "Most of the owners don't live here." His thin mouth twisted scornfully. "Look for them in Liberal, or Tyrone, or Guthrie. Highfalutin citizens, most of them. Don't want to get their hands dirty. Now mind you, there's a few fellows here who have their own little enterprises, but all of them leave keeping the peace up to me. That's the way I like it." He flexed the fingers of his gun hand as if exercising them.

"You mentioned details."

"That's right." Brandon eyed Clint as if he were looking over a prize stallion to add to his herd. "I ain't looking for any more enforcers. But this operation has gotten big, too big for one man to handle sometimes, especially since I got other business to tend to every now and then. I need a *segundo*, a right-hand man who can run things for me if need be, or step in and take charge when I can't be two places at once. I think I'm looking at that man.''

''You're putting a powerful lot of faith in a hombre you met just last night.''

''I don't think so.'' Brandon paused. ''Some of my boys have seen you before, and they vouch for you being who you say you are. And Clint Bradlock's got a rep as a straight shooter, the devil on wheels in any kind of scrap, and the best kind of man to have on your side when the odds go bad.'' He fell silent and waited for a response.

Clint mulled it over. He had no way of knowing if Brandon had anything to do with the robbery of Herns's gold shipment, but the gun boss seemed to have a hand in just about everything that went on in this sorry town. And even if he had no connection with the surviving robber, working as his *segundo* would give Clint a reason for staying in White City as well as the freedom he needed to poke around. But the Clint Bradlock of infamous reputation wouldn't take the job without knowing a little more.

''Let's talk about *dinero*,'' he suggested.

Brandon's smile was cynical. ''A man after my own heart. The owners give me some leeway in these things. Most of my boys just take what I pay them. But for you, I can manage something a little sweeter. I'll pay you top gun hand's wages, or let you in for a piece of the take. Your choice.''

''What's yours?''

Again the predatory smile flashed. "I get a percentage of the take."

"I reckon that's my choice too."

"I thought it might be," Brandon said with obvious satisfaction. "I get five percent. If I hold their feet to the fire a little bit, the owners will go along with another two-and-a-half percent for you."

"Deal," Clint said.

"Good. I have a feeling you'll like Beer City." Brandon looked past Clint toward the stairway. His eyes narrowed just a fraction.

Clint followed the direction of his gaze. The seductive redhead he had noticed at Brandon's side last night was just coming down the stairs. She wore a tight, low-cut gown that was fancier than any of the other bar girls' outfits that Clint had seen around. Her red hair reminded him of a fiery sunset on the prairie. Worn loose, it fell to her shoulders and shimmered as she moved.

She hurried to Brandon and pressed her full figure intimately against him. Clint couldn't hear the words she murmured in his ear.

Brandon swatted her seat lightly, then eased her back gently. "Clint, meet Rhonda. You might say she's my private stock." His leer was suggestive.

Clint touched the brim of his hat. Rhonda spared him little more than a nod. Her face was fetching, but Clint could see a hardness to the set of her mouth beneath the makeup. Her eyes had the age of experience.

She stepped back in close to Brandon and tiptoed to whisper to him again.

"Later, baby," Brandon told her with a chuckle. Once more he pressed her back. "Right now, I got to show my new *segundo* around our little community."

Rhonda took a step farther back from him on her own. She crossed her arms over the low-cut bodice of her dress. "Who are you going to see?" she snapped petulantly.

Brandon's sudden frown was dark and threatening. "You just be here for me when I come back," he growled. "Got that, honey?"

She quailed beneath his glare. "Sure, sure, baby," she promised breathlessly. "I'm sorry. I didn't mean—"

"Let's go, Clint," Brandon cut her off coldly. He all but shouldered her aside as he headed for the door.

She dropped her head as Clint passed her. He couldn't read her face. He caught a whiff of her heady perfume.

At the door, Brandon paused and glanced back. The long gun hand whom Clint had noticed earlier had risen and was following in their wake. Brandon ignored Rhonda, and nodded at the gun slick. "Quick Handley," he introduced the fellow. "My new watchdog. He's a good man. Done some important jobs for me."

Clint exchanged nods with him. Handley was thin and had a hard, narrow face. His nickname might have come from his eyes, which darted about beneath his narrow brow, or from his hand, which twitched near the pearl-handled butt of his long-barreled Colt.

Paying him no more heed, Brandon stalked out of the saloon. Clint followed, conscious of Handley scuttling after them.

Clint drew even with Brandon. "Pretty little sorrel mare back there," he commented.

Brandon glanced at him sharply. "For now, she's private stock, like I said," he warned. Then he shook his head ruefully. "Trouble with her is, sometimes she gets to thinking it's the other way around. No woman owns me." He broke off and lifted his chin to indicate a wagon just pulling into the edge of town. "Some of the working girls just arriving. Bunch of them live over in Liberal, where the accommodations are a mite better. They pay a driver to haul them back and forth every day."

The wagon was loaded with at least a dozen garishly painted women of varying ages. A few of them waved or called out to the cowhands and lowlifes loitering on the dirt street. The wagon pulled to a halt, and they disembarked as they straightened their shabby finery and chattered and laughed among themselves.

The wagon driver was a sodden, slovenly fellow packing a sawed-off double-barreled shotgun beside him on the seat. He nodded deferentially to Brandon.

The women quickly dispersed toward the various dance halls and saloons housed in tents and ramshackle frame buildings. Some of the tents needed patching, and nearly all of the buildings needed a coat of paint.

There was no boardwalk, which meant that, during the spring and late summer downpours that swept over the plains, the whole town would become a muddy mire.

Clint cut a glance at Brandon, whose gait had become an arrogant saunter. He was gazing about the squalid community like a monarch strolling through his kingdom. His thumb was hooked easily in his gun belt near his exotic pistol. He used his left hand to gesture at a two-story building a little more prepossessing than most.

"Yellow Snake Saloon," he identified it. "A gal named Nell Moriarty runs the house upstairs." He gave a snort of ugly humor. "Town did have a marshal once, until Nell pumped a load of buckshot into his hide. He was just a no-account rustler, anyway."

"No laws," Clint said. "But what are the rules?"

"The owners don't like for too many customers to get killed," Brandon explained. "Bad for business. The dead ones can't spend their money, and the killings run off some of the live ones who can. If two men want to fight, that's okay just so long as it doesn't involve innocent bystanders. The street's the place for them to settle their differences. If some of the customers get too rowdy and go to tearing a place up, the best thing is to bust their heads and try not to kill anybody in the process. My enforcers do most of that sort of work. It's just routine. We got cribs in back of a few places like the Elephant to let the drunks sleep it off, and con men and pickpockets aren't allowed to work over anyone who's had too much to drink. If a man causes too much trouble or kills too much, even in fair fights, he's told to leave.''

Clint thought of the gambler Rancon and his senseless, vicious grin. "Seems simple enough," he said aloud.

"It is simple," Brandon said. "The hard part is staying alive.''

Their course had taken them almost to the edge of town. A bedraggled group of cowboys were just riding out. They held their horses to a careful walk, as if each step hurt their heads. *Headed back to their herd,* Clint figured. Another gaggle of cowpokes was arriving at an eager gallop to take their places. They pounded past with jeers at their departing comrades.

Brandon grinned after them. "Cash on the hoof," he remarked with pleasure. "Come on, I'll show you one more thriving enterprise in our fair community.''

A line of low trees marked a creek bed just beyond the outermost limits of the town. Brandon led the way down a rutted wagon track that disappeared into the trees.

"We try to keep as many things local as we can," he said over his shoulder. " 'Course, a few of the girls come from Liberal, and we have to haul in some of the beer and liquor for the saloons. But lots of it we produce right here at home on Hog Creek.''

Muddy water moved slowly in the creek bed under the shadows of the trees. It took Clint a moment to make out a big wooden lean-to in front of the mouth of a cave. A large pile of firewood stood nearby.

Movement stirred in the cave mouth. A bearded, pasty-skinned man in overalls emerged from the gloom like a ghoul out of a crypt. He held a big, old Sharps buffalo gun across his chest. From behind him came a muffled gurgling.

"Oh, it's you, Mr. Brandon," the pale man said with a whiskey-roughened voice.

"Just taking a look around, Lester," Brandon reassured him. "How's production?"

Lester bared scraggly fangs in a smile. "She's going right good, Mr. Brandon." He turned briefly back into the lean-to. "Here, you want a taste?" He hefted a gallon jug eagerly.

"Don't mind if I do." Brandon took the jug, propped it on a crooked arm with the practiced ease of an old-time mountain man, and took a gulp of its contents. Snorting, he lowered the jug.

"Mighty good 'shine, Lester," he praised hoarsely, and then passed the jug to Quick Handley. The gun hand tilted it to his lips for a sip, shuddered, then handed it on to Clint. The bare scent of it was fiery. *Bottled dynamite,* Clint thought. He passed it back to Lester.

"We'll water it down, bottle it, and sell it," Brandon explained to Clint. "Cheaper than having it hauled in."

Clint guessed there were other men in the cave who operated the still. He had an unsettling mental image of more beings like Lester, laboring down in the stifling gloom to produce this devil's brew.

"We have to keep the still guarded," Brandon said

as they left. "Not many of the customers know it's here, but every now and then some cowpoke or rummy takes a notion to steal a free sample. Lester had to plug one with that buffalo rifle a couple of weeks back. He won't be stealing nothing now."

"Another rule?" Clint observed dryly.

Brandon laughed harshly. "That's right. Don't steal the whiskey!"

Clint glanced back once as they withdrew from the creek. Lester had disappeared into his crypt.

Back at the edge of town, Brandon suddenly drew to a halt and raised his voice in a shout. "Yo, Ratter!"

A skulking figure detached itself from the shadows on the other side of the street and scuttled toward them. Clint saw that it was the shifty-eyed little man who had been his shadow the night before.

Ratter halted and peered up at Brandon. "Yessir, Mr. Brandon?"

"Make the rounds," Brandon ordered. "Tell the boys and the barkeeps that I got me a new *segundo*." He clapped Clint on the shoulder. "Clint Bradlock here. Nobody bucks him. You make that clear. Understand?"

Ratter stared at Clint with wide eyes. Even vermin like Ratter knew his name, Clint reflected with disgust. Maybe the thought showed on his face. Ratter backed away from him.

"I'll see to it, Mr. Brandon. Don't you worry." He scurried hurriedly down the street.

Brandon stared after him for a moment. "He'll get

the word out,'' he assured Clint. He produced a hip flask from his back pocket and threw down a sip from it. ''I'll show you my house now.''

The structure to which he led them was at the far end of town from the still on Hog Creek. It was the only true house, and easily the finest building in town. Two stories high, painted white, with a wraparound porch, it boasted stately columns in front. As was usual with fancy territorial homes, it was built with high ceilings and plenty of windows to allow the prairie breeze to circulate.

Light-blue lace curtains fluttered in the windows, and Clint saw a vase of purple cowboy roses on a front windowsill. He managed not to glance at Brandon in surprise. Was the boss of Beer City a married man? Clint couldn't quite picture the worldly Rhonda occupying this stately home.

''Had it built myself,'' Brandon boasted. ''Furnished it with the best that money could buy from back East.''

As they passed through the small gate in the neat picket fence, a big man rose easily from a chair on the front porch. Clint recognized him as the boxer he had seen sparring alone in the public fight ring when he rode into town. A glass mug of beer and a gleaming sawed-off double-barreled shotgun were within easy reach on a side table. He came down the steps with the light movements of a puma.

Up close, his brawny form was impressive. He topped Clint by a couple of inches. His broad face bore the wear and tear that Clint had seen before on men who made their living in the prizefight ring. Despite the heat, he wore a tattered, colorless stocking cap pulled down on his skull.

"Sledger, say howdy to Clint Bradlock." Brandon turned to Clint. "Sledger does some special body-guarding for me." He stepped back a pace. His eyes were hard and watchful.

"Bradlock, huh?" Sledger sounded as though he had taken a solid blow to the throat at some point in his career. If Clint's name disquieted him, he didn't show it. He shot out a big hand almost as if he were throwing a body blow in the ring.

Clint clasped hands with him, and instantly his fingers felt as though they were being stepped on by a horse. Sweat popped out on his forehead. He gripped back hard, feeling the muscles knot in his forearm. Sledger didn't change expression, and his grip didn't slacken. For several heartbeats they stood toe-to-toe, hands locked.

Clint looked into the small, hard eyes beneath the craggy, scarred brows. "Tell me when the fight starts," he gritted. He would kill this big lummox before he let him cripple his gun hand.

Abruptly the pressure eased. "You'll know when," Sledger answered him, and gave a harsh chuckle. It sounded like rocks rattling together.

"I'd lay odds on you over Sledger if you were facing off with six-guns," Brandon said. "But if it ever came to fists, I'd have to put my money on Sledger. He's a prizefighter. We stage some bouts here in White City, and Sledger sometimes just takes on all comers. Never seen him beat, not in a pickup fight or by another pro. He scrambled one poor cowpoke's brains so bad that he ain't much use for nothing now except sweeping out the saloons.''

''Could be, your luck's due to run out,'' Clint said coldly.

''Don't bet your pistol on it, gunfighter.'' Sledger rolled his head about on his thick neck and shifted his weight from foot to foot as if about to come out of his corner for the first round. ''Remember, I fight tonight, boss,'' he rumbled without looking away from Clint. ''I'll need somebody to look after things here.''

''Clint will take care of it,'' Brandon told him. Then he addressed Clint. ''Sledger is bodyguard for my ward. This house is for her more than it's for me. Most nights, I stay over at the Elephant.''

''Your ward?'' Clint asked.

''My foster brother's daughter. When he died, he named me to look out for her. It's all legal. She was away at school back East until a year ago. When she finished and came out here, I had this house built for her.''

Before Clint could respond, the front door of the house opened and a young woman stepped hesitantly onto the porch.

''Carter,'' she said in a pleasant voice, ''may I get you and the other gentlemen some refreshments?''

Clint saw Brandon's nostrils flare possessively as he

looked at her. She was worth looking at. Her comely figure was clad in a modest blue dress. She had black hair done up with a matching blue ribbon above warm, pretty features that made the breath catch in Clint's throat. Here in the depravity of White City, she was like a flower in a town dump.

"Some whiskey out on the porch would be fine, honey," Brandon told her.

She murmured an acknowledgment and disappeared into the house. Clint fancied that her eyes brushed his just as she turned away.

She reappeared by the time they had seated themselves at a round table near the end of the porch. Out of the edge of his vision, Clint watched her graceful movements as she set an unopened bottle in the center of the table and placed a shot glass in front of each of them. He caught a faint, sweet scent as she reached past him to set his glass before him. Brandon and Sledger kept their unblinking eyes fixed on her, Clint noted. Her lovely face was flushed by the time she straightened up from the table.

"Elaine, this here's Clint Bradlock," Brandon said before she could depart. "He'll be spelling Sledger some in watching over the house. Clint, meet Miss Elaine Allison, my ward."

Clint rose and doffed his Stetson. "My pleasure," he said to her across the table. He glimpsed the trace of a sneer on Sledger's thick lips.

"Nice to meet you." She gave a little curtsy. For an instant her eyes seemed to touch his again. Then she backed away from the table and bowed her head demurely. "I'll be inside if you need me, Carter." Clint imagined that she had hesitated just slightly before speaking her guardian's name.

"Thanks, honey." Brandon's gaze followed her until the door closed on her back. Then he swung his head toward Clint. "Sledger guards her most of the time, but when he isn't watching after her, she's your responsibility. You're to see that nothing happens to her, because I've got plans for her future. I found an old squaw to live with her and look after her needs. Elaine's sweet and decent and innocent, not like the floozies at the dance halls and saloons here. I won't have her associating with riffraff. And she's off-limits to you too, Bradlock," he added sternly. "You stay out of the house. If need be, you bunk over there." He indicated a small shed at the end of the house. "You savvy what I'm saying to you?"

"I savvy," Clint said.

Brandon gave a sharp nod of satisfaction. His dark eyes were hard. He reached for the whiskey bottle.

The sound of a piano floated to them through the open window. Brandon cocked his head to listen. "That's her," he said proudly.

The tune was bright and cheerful, but it sounded too fast to Clint's ear. It was almost as if its gaiety was forced. What in tarnation, he brooded, was a girl like Elaine Allison doing in Beer City?

Chapter Four

From where he sat on the front porch of Brandon's house, Clint could hear the sounds of the crowd that had gathered to watch the fight. He couldn't see the ring, but he guessed that the evening's bout had started. He hoped sourly that Sledger had finally met his match. His hand still ached from the prizefighter's crushing grip that morning.

He had spent the rest of the day prowling the town on his own, letting himself be seen, keeping his ears open. He had not learned anything to help him in his quest, but Brandon's minion, Ratter, had apparently gotten the word out, as Brandon had predicted. The barkeeps, dance hall girls, and enforcers all treated him with respect and caution.

In one saloon he had seen Rancon at a corner table. The cardsharp's only opponent was himself. He was playing solitaire, maybe because his eagerness to settle disputes with gunfire had robbed him of players willing to match cards with him. Rancon had spotted him and smiled his meaningless smile in empty acknowledgment. Clint had left him to his game.

Several bar girls had winked or smiled suggestively at him as he passed. A couple had been even more bold in their suggestions. Apparently the idea of being the new *segundo*'s woman was an appealing one. Clint brushed them aside as politely as he could. His mind kept conjuring an image of Elaine Allison's lovely features and raven-black hair.

He frowned now on the porch, and wondered again about the circumstances that had brought her to White City as the legal ward of Carter Brandon. The gun boss's terse explanation had raised more questions than it had answered.

Down in the center of town by the fight ring, several bonfires had been started so that the crowd could see the combatants. The flames cast dim, shifting illumination over the porch. The crowd would be a rough one, he reflected. Any crowd made up of White City's denizens would be a bloodthirsty pack to begin with, and a brutal slugfest in the ring would only fuel their savagery. Add the rotgut whiskey from Hog Creek, and disputes over wagers on the fight, and there would no doubt be even more bodies than on the night before. Brandon's enforcers would have their hands full unless he missed his guess.

A few notes of piano music floated out of the house. Clint cocked an ear as the playing gathered strength. It was a lilting, pleasant piece that clashed with the distant, ugly murmurings of the crowd. A lot like the player herself, Clint thought.

He imagined her sitting, graceful and poised, before a fine piano, her fingers dancing over the keys. He hadn't seen her since coming on duty to replace Sledger. He took an odd pleasure at this confirmation of her nearness.

As the piece ended, he shook his head to clear it. He had all but drifted into a reverie under the spell of her playing. *Some bodyguard,* he chided himself.

As she launched immediately into another melody, he pushed himself up from his chair and descended the steps softly. He needed to check out the rest of the property if he was to take his bodyguarding duties seriously.

He prowled the boundaries of the yard and stuck his head inside the shack where Elaine's guard was to bunk. He guessed this was Sledger's regular quarters. The interior was shabby and smelled of old sweat.

As he withdrew, the sound of the crowd swelled briefly to a roar. One of the pugilists must have landed a good blow. He realized abruptly that the piano playing had stopped. In that same moment, the voice of Elaine Allison was raised in a scream of fear and outrage.

Clint whipped his .45 from leather and raced to the rear corner of the house. He stepped fast and wide around it, straining to pierce the gloom with his searching gaze. The back door stood open. Light was streaming from it. Clint charged forward, then drew up short just outside the illumination. Only a fool or a tenderfoot rushed in blind on danger.

The lock on the door had been smashed, and from inside came a muffled cry and the scuffling of feet. Something fell and broke.

"Just you settle down, gal," a man's coarse voice ordered. "We're here to have us a little fun. This beats watching some fight. We knew that with old Sledger in the ring, you'd be sitting here sweet and sassy waiting for us. Ow!" He cursed. An open hand struck flesh.

Clint went through the door, gun in fist. He found himself in a hallway. He covered its length in a half dozen strides and burst into a parlor.

"Get your hands off her!" he snarled.

The scene in front of him locked rigid for a startled instant. A broken whiskey bottle lay on the floor. Three slovenly men, pistols holstered at their sides, had Elaine trapped against a grand piano that all but filled one corner of the room. The burly fellow gripping her shoulder had one open hand uplifted as if to strike. Helpless in his grip, Elaine still glared up at him with terrified defiance. A hand mark stood out redly on her white cheek.

The tableau broke as her captor swung a bearded face around to peer over his shoulder. His eyes were murderous. The man next to him spat out an oath and spun about, grabbing for his holstered gun.

Tenderfoot's move, Clint thought, and he shot him square in the body, the Colt bucking in his hand. Its roar in the confined room was like the clap of open palms over his ears. The rowdy flopped back onto the piano, then slid to the floor, groaning.

Through the veil of powder smoke Clint saw the third fellow throw up his hands. Elaine's captor whirled, trapping Elaine in front of him as a shield. One thick arm was around her throat. He towered a good head above her. Clint snapped his arm out straight, easing the hammer back. He aimed down the .45's barrel right between those murderous eyes. He didn't speak. He intended to kill the man, and he guessed his intentions were plain on his face.

The big rowdy paled, and he thrust Elaine away from him and jerked up his hands. Fear had replaced the savagery in his eyes. His companion still stood with his arms raised in surrender. Clint's finger was tight on the trigger.

"Don't kill us, mister," the big man quavered.

Clint eased up on the trigger. "How does this town hold a trial?" he asked coolly.

The big rowdy's knees actually buckled a little. "By the saints, don't turn us over to Brandon! He'd hang us for sure!"

"No more than you deserve," Clint said.

The wounded man was sitting up, holding his middle. Out of his side vision, Clint could see Elaine. The back of one hand was raised to her mouth. She was watching the scene with wide eyes.

"Take your pard and get out of here," Clint growled. "Leave your guns. The Good Book says wrath will come upon you. Well, if you come back to

White City, it sure will. I'll drill you as soon as I lay eyes on you. Brandon won't need to hang you.''

The big man and his buddy obeyed. They hauled their wounded companion to his feet, and supporting him between them, they lumbered clumsily from the room. Clint watched from the hallway until they disappeared out the back door. Automatically he replaced the spent shell in the Colt.

As he stepped back into the parlor, a withered figure stirred in the gloom of a doorway. Clint saw a bent and gnarled old Indian woman lurking there. In one bony hand she gripped a huge bowie knife every bit as deadly as his own. For a moment he stared at her. She met his gaze with unblinking black eyes that he could read about as well as he could read a stone. She made a movement, and somehow the huge knife disappeared from sight into her shabby buckskin dress. Clint recalled Brandon's reference to an old squaw who lived in the house. It seemed Elaine hadn't been quite as undefended as he had thought.

A soft moan brought his attention back to Elaine. She had not moved from where she stood other than to lower her hand away from her mouth. She swayed slightly.

Quickly he crossed the room and reached out for her. Then she caught herself with an obvious effort of will and straightened resolutely. Clint's hands were almost touching her shoulders. Awkwardly he drew back.

''Thank you,'' she said softly. ''I'm all right now.''

Clint thought that she still looked shaken. "You'd better sit down," he suggested, more gruffly than he'd intended.

She nodded and sank onto a plush couch. For the first time, Clint noted that she was wearing a different dress from the one he had seen that morning. It was yellow as a canary and had a high neck. A matching ribbon set off the ebony of her hair.

The old Indian appeared at Clint's side like a ghost. For a moment she regarded Elaine silently. "I get tea for Miss Elaine," she announced. With one last unreadable glance at Clint, she shuffled out of the room.

Clint became aware that Elaine was gazing up at him with intense blue eyes. "I'm glad you let them go," she said quietly.

Clint stared in surprise at her remark.

"Oh, I know they need to be tried and punished," she hurried on, her tone as intense as her eyes. "But Carter wouldn't give them a trial. He'd just hang them in front of everyone." A shudder raced over her, and she dropped her gaze. "It happened once before." Clint could barely hear her words. "A man tried to— to bother me, and Sledger caught him. It was terrible. He beat him and kept on beating him even when the man was helpless. I begged him to stop, but he just ignored me. When Uncle Carter arrived, he had his gunmen drag the man out and hang him. He said the town needed to learn a lesson." She shook her head miserably at the memory. "I always felt the whole matter was somehow my fault."

"It was his own fault for attacking you," Clint said sharply.

"I know," she admitted. "It's just that this town is so awful and violent. There's no law except what Uncle Carter says there is." She looked up at him again and managed a small smile. "My manners are awful. I haven't even thanked you for coming to my rescue. Please sit down. Forgive me for not standing. I still feel a little weak."

Uncomfortable with the situation, Clint seated himself at the far end of the couch from her. The couch suddenly seemed much smaller. Vaguely he recollected Brandon's warning that the house was off-limits.

She turned about slightly to face him. "Your name's Clint Bradlock, isn't it?"

"Yes, ma'am," Clint mumbled. He felt a twinge of relief that his name didn't seem to mean anything to her. He took off his hat. He wasn't used to keeping company with lovely and respectable young women.

"Call me Elaine, please." She lowered her eyes demurely. "I'm glad it was you, not Sledger, who was guarding me. I could tell this morning, when Carter introduced you, that you were different from the others here. You're not a pagan or an outlaw."

Cold, skeletal fingers touched Clint's nape. Could she see through his facade so easily? If she could, then who else hereabouts might do the same thing? It was a disquieting thought.

He noted that the red mark from her attacker's slap was fading, but that a warm flush now suffused her face. He understood that her emotions were still running high, and that she wasn't guarding her words as she normally might have done.

The old Indian woman glided into the room. She set a tray with two cups of tea on the coffee table before the couch. Clint glanced about the parlor with more care. It was as elegantly furnished as Brandon had boasted. The furniture was all oak and mahogany. A tall bookcase was filled with leather-bound volumes, and a large Bible lay open on a reading table beside an upholstered chaise lounge near the window.

The old woman faded silently from the room. Elaine gazed fondly after her. "Sweet Vieja," she said almost to herself. "Carter found her to stay with me after that other incident. She's a dear soul, even if she does look like a savage."

Vieja, Clint mused. The name meant old woman in Spanish. It was fitting.

"She must like you, or she wouldn't have brought you tea," Elaine commented and then broke off, as if realizing that her words might be improper.

Clint looked quickly away and reached for the tea. She did the same. Her soft hand brushed his. She murmured a quick apology. The tea was not too hot, and sweet. The parlor was making him warm.

Her earlier words came back to him. "Carter Brandon's your uncle?" he asked.

"Oh, no, that's just what I've called him since I was a child. I still do sometimes, even though he likes me to call him by his first name now. I don't really feel comfortable doing that. He's my legal guardian since my father died. My grandparents took Uncle Carter in as an orphan, and raised him just like he was a younger brother to my father. When he got older, he became some kind of a range detective or something, and he'd come by and see us occasionally on our farm. He was always nice to me when I was a little girl.'' She smiled faintly at her memories.

"What happened to your parents?" Clint asked. He found her story strangely gripping.

Her tone saddened. "Mama died several years ago, and then Papa sent me back East to school. He said he wanted me to grow up to be a lady. I was in school when he died last year. In his will he named Carter as my guardian. He didn't have any other relatives. Carter saw to it that I finished school, and then he had me come out here.'' She fell silent, and her smooth brow furrowed in a frown. "He's different from what I remember," she added.

"Do you plan on staying here when he's no longer your guardian?" For some reason the question's answer seemed very important to Clint.

Elaine sipped at her tea. "I don't know. I don't want to be disloyal to Uncle—I mean, to Carter—after all he's done for me, but I just don't see how he can live in this terrible place. There's no church, or school, or families, or anything a real town has. I know Carter had this big house built for me, but I don't have any friends here except Vieja. I get so lonely sometimes that I don't think I can stand it any longer. Most of the time I spend reading my Bible or my other books, and playing the piano.'' Her voice trailed off sadly.

Clint felt awkward suddenly, and he prepared to get to his feet. ''Well, I guess I'd better check and see that those hombres really did hightail it out of town.''

She stood up quickly as he rose, so that for a moment they were very close together. He smelled the sweet scent that he had caught that afternoon. Then she drew back slightly. He settled his Stetson on his head.

''Thank you so much,'' she said. ''I hope I'll get to see you again. I can't talk to Sledger as I can to you.'' As if on impulse, she reached out and touched his hand fleetingly. Then she pulled her fingers quickly back.

''I'll be around here,'' Clint promised. ''I'll see about getting somebody to repair that back door.''

''Okay.'' She moved aside to let him pass.

In the hallway he had the sensation of other eyes on him. He wondered if Vieja was watching him from some dark recess.

Outside, there was no sign of the rowdies, and no alarm had been raised. The sound of his shot had been muffled by the walls of the house and must not have carried above the sounds of the crowd, he calculated. Besides, stray shots were common in White City.

Her farewell seemed to echo softly in his ears, and he could still feel the soft touch of her hand. He hoped he would get to see her again too.

But he saw her only once, from a distance, over the next two days. On the morning after the attack, she was on the porch talking to Brandon, and they seemed to be arguing.

Brandon had not been pleased over his handling of the rowdies. "You should have killed all three of them," he told Clint savagely. "Or held them to be hanged."

Clint shrugged. "Maybe next time."

Brandon had let it drop.

Sledger had won his fight, and Clint wasn't called on to replace him again. As Brandon's second-in-command, he discovered, he had little to do for the most part. Since just about anything went in White City, and the regular enforcers were on patrol to keep matters in hand, he was able to do pretty much as he pleased. His reputation made most of the hired guns stay clear of him, and so he kept to himself, moving from bar to bar, listening to the flow of talk among the saddle tramps and cowpokes.

In a shabby tent saloon on the second night after Sledger's fight, he saw Rancon again. The cardsharp was gazing broodingly from his solitaire game toward two gun hawks sharing a bottle at a nearby table. Clint wondered why the gambler was still hanging around town. A drooling, slack-jawed fellow was raking the dirt floor. Was he Sledger's hapless victim?

The bar itself was nothing more than a wide plank set on barrels. Clint shook his head at the barkeep and eased down the bar closer to the two gunmen. He recognized them as some of Brandon's enforcers and guessed they were off duty.

"Brandon's planning another one," he caught one fellow's words.

His companion replied, but Clint couldn't hear what he said. It sounded disparaging.

"Maybe so," the first man countered. "But the pay's mighty good for riding with him. Makes the risk worthwhile, I say."

Their voices dropped to mutters. Clint glanced at Rancon. In the uncertain light of the tent's single lantern, the gambler's face was cruel and predatory. He appeared to sense Clint's gaze, and shifted his eyes to him. He grinned his feral grin and flicked a card faceup on the table.

"Care for a hand?" His tone was sardonic.

"No, thanks. Your opponents keep dying."

Rancon quirked an eyebrow and turned another card without looking at it. "Maybe they've just had bad luck."

"I don't think I'll try the odds that mine's any better."

Rancon shifted his shoulders indifferently. He didn't seem to be disturbed at losing a potential mark. He looked toward the enforcers, but they were just rising. Rancon scowled and turned his attention back to his cards.

The two gunmen drifted out into the darkness, still talking in low tones. Rancon didn't look up again. Clint left the bar and stepped outside after them.

The pair had paused a short distance away to roll cigarettes. Clint drew into the shadows, waiting for them to move on. After a few moments they sauntered off. Clint stirred, but before he could follow them, Rancon slipped out of the saloon and headed in the opposite direction. He hadn't seen Clint and he didn't look behind him.

Clint hesitated. There was something furtive in the gambler's manner, and he bore watching, Clint decided. He cat footed after the man.

Rancon made his way toward the edge of town. Only once did he glance back, and Clint froze in the darkness. Rancon continued, and at last he halted in front of a dance hall where he was joined by another man. Clint recognized the jerky movements of Quick Handley. What was Brandon's pet gunfighter doing with the likes of Rancon?

As the two men moved on, Clint ghosted after them, staying to the shadows. A voice shouted drunkenly, then fell silent. A woman's vulgar laugh came from an alley. Raucous music blasted from one of the honky-tonks. Clint thought of Elaine Allison. The elegant parlor of the house in which Brandon had installed her seemed to be in another world. Clint shook the distracting image from his mind.

Rancon and Handley disappeared into the leaning shape of an abandoned shack at the end of one of the ominous side streets. They had left the livelier part of town behind them. Clint paused and frowned into the gloom. A feeble glow sprang from the shed's single window. Someone inside had lit a lantern.

As Clint started forward again, he felt a faint vibration underfoot, and then hoofbeats sounded from out on the prairie and soon the centaur shape of a rider pulled to a halt in front of the shack. Clint crept forward like a lynx.

The door opened as the newcomer stepped onto the sagging porch. In the brief wash of light, Clint saw that the stranger was Buck, the lean gunfighter whom Brandon had fired for failing to cover his back against the old prospector.

Stepping cautiously, Clint approached the shed. If he spooked Buck's horse, it might alert the trio to his presence. As he drew near the window, a shadow moved within, and a shade was drawn over the yellow square of light.

Clint pressed close to the flimsy board wall beside the window. He could hear the muffled voices of the men inside, but he couldn't make out the words. There didn't seem to be anyone else present, just the three dangerous men meeting like conspirators in secret. Obviously Buck hadn't gone far when he left town. Just as obviously, he and the gambler and Quick Handley were up to something.

Silently Clint withdrew. The risk of discovery was too great for him to stay and wait for their clandestine meeting to end. Placing his feet carefully, he moved back toward the lights and babble of the main street.

As he passed the entrance of a ramshackle gambling den, a voice hailed him. His nerves still taut, he turned sharply and saw the streak of fear race across the shifty face of Ratter as he emerged from the den.

Clint forced himself to relax. ''Yeah?'' he demanded curtly.

Ratter swallowed hard. ''Mr. Brandon wants you over to the Elephant. I been looking for you.''

''Thanks.''

Ratter fled back into the gambling house. Clint headed up the street toward the saloon. He found it going full blast. Tinny music battered his ears. The stench of carousing men filled his nostrils.

He spotted Brandon with Rhonda at a corner table, and made his way through the press, flicking his eyes about the saloon. Three women danced on the stage. A gun hand lounging at the bar seemed to be filling Handley's role as Brandon's watchdog.

Brandon flashed white teeth in a smile of greeting. ''Pull up a chair, Clint.'' He poured whiskey for himself and Rhonda.

Clint nodded at the bottle as he sat. ''That come from Hog Creek?'' he inquired wryly.

Brandon snorted. ''Not very likely. This is imported.'' He chuckled and savored the whiskey. Rhonda spared Clint no more than a glance. She was staring at Brandon with smoldering eyes and leaning provocatively toward him.

Clint gestured at the new watchdog. ''You get rid of Handley?''

''Naw.'' Brandon shook his head. ''He had a little filly down the street he had a hankering to see. He got one of the boys to cover here for him.''

Clint didn't question it. He leaned back in his chair and tilted his Stetson up slightly. "What've you got?"

"I'll be leaving town tomorrow," Brandon told him after a moment. "Likely be gone two or three days. I'm taking a handful of the boys with me."

"Business?"

Brandon glanced sharply at him. "Yeah. You'll be in charge while I'm gone. And there's one other thing."

"What's that?"

Brandon looked away. "Elaine's been pestering me to let her get out of the house ever since that trouble the other night. She wants to go for a ride or something. I haven't had time to go with her, and this deal I've got to handle can't be put off. I told her I'd take her out when I got back, but she doesn't want to wait." His thin lips twisted.

Abruptly, Rhonda pushed her chair back and rose to her feet. Words seemed ready to burst out of her, but Brandon gave her a flat look from his dark eyes that kept her silent. Her full lips were trembling, and tears were starting to mar the mascara around her eyes. She stepped back from the table, turned, and flounced away.

Brandon stared broodingly after her. He filled his shot glass and emptied it with a snap of his wrist. "Sledger can't sit a horse worth a darn," he went on as if the interruption hadn't occurred. "I know I can trust you with Elaine, since you didn't take advantage of her the other night. I want you to go riding with her tomorrow afternoon. Sledger can look after things here for a couple of hours.''

''Sounds better than ramrodding gunfighters and policing drunks,'' Clint allowed.

Brandon's gaze was hooded as he said, ''Just don't go getting any wrong ideas, Bradlock.''

Chapter Five

Sledger rose to his feet from his customary place on the porch as Clint reined in his paint at the gate. The prizefighter stared sullenly from beneath his stocking cap at the little mare on the lead rope. Clint had selected her for Elaine from Brandon's private string.

Sledger shifted his small, mean eyes to Clint. "What do you think you're doing?" he rasped from down in his throat.

"Fixing to take Miss Allison for a ride." Clint gauged the big man's hostility. There looked to be something more to it than the mutual dislike festering between them. "Brandon said he'd told you about it."

Sledger grunted. "I told him I didn't think it was a good idea."

"Guess he doesn't listen to you." Clint tossed the words back at him. "Too bad you ain't much of a horseman."

Sledger's big fists clenched and he took a step forward. For a moment, Clint thought he would come down from the porch after him, and he tensed to wheel his paint out of the way.

The door to the house opened and Elaine appeared. The bright smile on her face faltered as she took in the two men eyeing each other. Then she came toward them determinedly. "Clint, I'm so glad you're here. I've got some snacks for us." She indicated the picnic basket and folded blanket on one arm. "Sledger, I'll be back in time for dinner. All right?" She leveled a disarming smile at him.

Sledger mumbled a surly response and drew back from the edge of the porch.

Elaine bounced down the steps and through the gate. She wore a tan divided riding skirt, a crisp white blouse, and a pert little Stetson. Beneath the hat, her midnight tresses fell freely to her shoulders.

Clint started to dismount and assist her, but she waved him back into his saddle. Quickly, she secured the quilt and picnic basket and then scrambled onto the mare. Astride, she settled her feet in the stirrups.

"Ready?" she asked brightly. Clint sensed an urgency in her to be away from the big house and her sullen bodyguard.

"Sure." He grinned. As he turned his horse, he had a glimpse of Sledger's little eyes fixed avidly on Elaine's mounted figure.

He put heels to the paint. Elaine drew the mare even with him a moment later and they moved out at a canter. Clint glanced back once as they headed onto the prairie. Sledger's towering form stood rigidly on the porch.

Elaine caught the direction of his glance. "Sledger can be so awful," she said with feeling. "It seems like he's always watching me. I wish Uncle Carter would have somebody else guard the house."

"Have you told him that?"

She nodded. "He won't listen. He says everyone in White City is scared of Sledger. And he trusts him because Sledger is scared of him. I think Uncle Carter really might be the only man Sledger is afraid to face."

Clint found himself wanting to make some fool's vow to protect her. He reined in the impulse and watched her riding beside him. Moving with her horse in a flowing rhythm, she was a far cry from the soiled doves in White City's dens of iniquity.

"You won't need to fret about Sledger this afternoon," he told her.

She flashed him a smile. "I know. It's so wonderful to be away from there for a while." She pushed her little Stetson back off her head to be held by its cord around her neck, and then pulled the dark mane of her hair out over it. She kicked her horse into a gallop. "Come on!" she called. Her smile was as warm and dazzling as the sunlight.

Clint kept pace with her. She threw her head back and let the wind of their passage blow through her hair so that it streamed out behind her. Clint had never seen a prettier sight.

Breathless at last, she pulled her mare to a walk. "That felt so good." Her eyes were sparkling as she looked out across the grassland rolling away from them. "This country just seems to go on forever, doesn't it?"

Clint thought that a trace of longing had crept into her voice. He forced himself to recall that they weren't too far out of White City. Danger, in the form of owlhoots or lawless saddle tramps, might be lurking over the next rise. But he didn't speak the thought aloud.

"Oh, look!" she exclaimed. She stopped her horse and pointed. "There's a prairie dog village!"

Clint followed her finger and saw the small telltale mounds that marked the animals' dens a couple of dozen yards distant. As he watched, two of the little creatures stuck their inquisitive heads up out of their mounds and peered quizzically in their direction. Then one of them popped the rest of the way out of its hole and scurried a short distance before sitting up on its haunches to gaze at them again. After a moment another one appeared, and what looked like a spirited game of tag started. The presence of the observers was apparently forgotten.

Clint couldn't resist glancing at Elaine. She was watching the display with a delighted smile. Clint's horse moved so that Clint's leg brushed hers. He wondered if she had noticed.

They rode on at a slower pace. A breeze played across the buffalo grass, setting it flowing in ripples up and down the hills. The sun shone bright and yellow in a blue sky lined with occasional white streaks of cloud.

"Where did you come from, Clint?" she asked presently without looking at him. "Why are you in White City?"

Wariness rose up in him. As he remembered her uncanny perceptions about him, he had the impulse to blurt out to her the whole truth of his purpose in White City. He trampled down the urge. To reveal his mission to anyone would be foolhardy.

"Your uncle needed a second-in-command," he made himself answer with a shrug.

Her small white teeth pressed into her lower lip. "You don't seem like the other men who work for Carter."

"Just get paid better."

She gave her head a quick shake. "No, it's more than that."

There was danger here. She could read him like an experienced tracker could read sign. "I've done a lot of things and been a lot of places," he said to distract her. He stuck to the truth as much as he could as he continued; it was easier that way. "I was a deputy marshal for a while. Then I tracked down wanted men for bounties. I even worked as a range detective for a time." That last came closest to the obscure and dangerous work he did for the Partners, he reflected somberly.

"And you never settled down?"

"Not so's you'd notice."

"You sound sad." Now she did look at him as she spoke.

Again she was reading him too well, sensing perhaps the loneliness of the wanderer who lived by his gun and his blade and his fists. "It's a good-enough life," he defended himself.

She pulled her gaze quickly from him. "Why did you start earning your living like this?"

"I was an orphan kid who was good with a gun and with my fists. It just seemed kind of natural to earn my money with them." His reputation had grown, and since his secret association with the Partners, it had been carefully nurtured. It seemed that he'd come too far down the trail of the gun to ever turn back now.

"Have you thought of doing something else?" She might have been reading his dark thoughts.

"Nothing much else I know how to do." And that was the truth also, he thought bleakly.

"You could try farming or ranching."

"Don't reckon I'm cut out for that kind of work," he said gruffly. It was something he had always told himself, and even believed. But now, sensing the sweetness of her spirit, he had the unexpected notion that, with a woman like her at his side, a man could make a go of just about anything the Good Lord gave him.

Disquieted, he looked away from her, scanning the skyline. Then he felt himself go tense suddenly.

"What is it?" Elaine asked quickly.

"Riders." Clint nodded toward the three horsemen silhouetted in the distance. He dropped a hand automatically to the butt of his Winchester in its saddle sheath.

Squinting, he watched the riders until they disappeared from view in the direction of White City. *Just some cowpokes headed for a good time,* he concluded. He drew his hand back from the Winchester.

Some of Elaine's gaiety had fled. "Uncle Carter told me once that he has big plans that don't include White City," she said as if to herself.

"What type of plans?"

She shrugged fetchingly. "I don't know. He didn't go into detail." She frowned. "But he said I'd make some man a good wife one day soon."

Clint felt a faint chill out there in the sunlight. What kind of plans did Brandon have for her? he wondered. "Does he leave town often?" he asked.

"Every few months." She added thoughtfully, "He never says much about where he's going."

"Got any notions?"

"He talks about business interests outside of White City, but I don't know what he means. Sometimes he leaves town with several of his men as he did this morning. He's been gone more often lately. And then there are times when I think he sends some of his men out to take care of his business for him." She was frowning as she spoke, as if she didn't want to guess at the nature of her guardian's business affairs.

It sounded as if Brandon might be leading or directing the raids against Howard Herns's holdings,

Clint speculated. But there seemed no good reason for him to single out Herns for his depredations.

Elaine shook her head as if ridding herself of unpleasant thoughts. "Let's forget about Uncle Carter and White City. I want to enjoy this afternoon."

Clint didn't argue. She had given him plenty to chew over and he was enjoying her presence. The sensation was one he didn't want to end.

They stopped at a small stand of cottonwoods near an old buffalo wallow that had retained some of the moisture from the heavy rains of spring and fall. Elaine dismounted and spread the brightly colored quilt on the soft grass in the shade of the cottonwoods. Then she delved in the picnic basket.

Clint sat his horse and watched her. Kneeling beside the open basket, she paused to look up at him. "Well, get off your horse!" she chided with a smile.

Clint dismounted and hunkered on his haunches while she unwrapped cold fried chicken and thick slices of homemade bread. Ready at last, she modestly tucked her legs beneath her skirt and reached to pat the quilt a discreet distance away. "Sit down."

Clint crossed his legs under him. He felt as though he shouldn't speak, because words might spoil this moment like a rock thrown into the clear reflection in a pond.

As they ate, she chattered about her school days back East and about her childhood on the farm. Once she paused to tilt her head and listen to the songbird that had settled in the branches of one of the cottonwoods overhead. Clint studied the smooth curve of her neck and the soft lines of her profile.

For dessert she had brought canned peaches, sweet and syrupy. When the last one was gone, she wiped her fingers neatly, placed her hands on the quilt behind her, and leaned back and closed her eyes. A stray ray of sunshine struck highlights from her ebony hair.

"Oh, I'd like to stay here forever," she whispered. "It's so peaceful and quiet and pleasant."

"They'll be sending search parties if we don't get started back right soon," Clint reminded her reluctantly.

She sighed and opened her eyes. "I know."

But she remained joyful as she packed the quilt and picnic basket.

As they rode, she hummed a tune that he recognized as a church hymn. The wordless melody seemed to float in the air. He resisted the urge to close his eyes and listen to it.

When the dark smudge of White City came into view on the horizon, she fell silent. "Thank you for putting up with me today," she said after a time.

"I hope I get to do it again," he said sincerely. He was surprised at how much he meant it.

She glanced at him quickly, and a blush touched her face. "I hope so too."

Nearing the town, Clint saw a small crowd of men clustered in front of a saloon just beyond the house. He picked out Sledger's burly shape looming above most of the others. The whole group seemed to shift expectantly as Clint reined up in front of the white picket fence. Clint frowned. He didn't like gatherings of this sort. Elaine seemed unaware of the tension.

Clint climbed off the paint and gave her a hand down, watching the crowd from the corner of his eye. They were the usual street sweepings and riffraff of White City. Elaine turned toward him as if to speak but, before she could, a ripple ran through the gathering, and a single figure was suddenly standing clear of the rest.

"Get inside!" Clint snapped.

Elaine blinked in surprise. "What?"

"You heard me. Get inside." Firmly Clint pushed her away from him.

She stared at him in bewilderment. "Why? What's happening?"

"Trouble," Clint said.

"Bradlock!" His shouted name cut off any response. For the first time she noted the ominous gathering and her eyes widened.

"Bradlock!" the lone figure shouted again. The voice tugged at Clint's memory. The other members of the crowd were moving back and away from the stranger now.

Elaine gave a little gasp and fled to the porch. Clint wanted her inside, but he had no time to fret about it.

"I heard you were here, Bradlock! I came looking for you!"

Clint felt a sad disgust down in his gut as the speaker came closer. He recognized the frail kid from the Blue

Belle Saloon in Guthrie. The Colt holstered at his side still looked too big for him.

"You're making a mistake, kid," Clint said loud enough to be heard.

"You made the mistake when you made me crawfish back in Guthrie!" The kid's voice was shrill. "I don't back down for no man, not even Clint Bradlock!"

"You'll live longer if you do." Clint moved sideways to be clear of the horses. A spooked horse could kill him as sure as a bullet from the kid's Colt.

"I been waiting for you!" The kid stopped some thirty feet distant. "They told me you'd be coming back."

Whiskey and the goadings of the crowd had driven him to a killing fever, Clint realized. "You couldn't let it ride," he tried regretfully one last time. He already knew it wasn't going to work. There was death in the kid's eyes—his own or Clint's.

"I still say you ain't man enough to take me."

A resigned coldness settled in Clint's soul. He stood poised, muscles only a little tense, as he had done so many times before. "Let's see," he said.

The kid's hand snapped toward his Colt. Clint's gun came up without thought, without planning, almost without effort. He was firing by the time he realized fully it was in his grip. The kid's gun fired too—down into the street between his boots. Clint cocked and fired again, coldly, because you didn't take chances against a man with his gun out.

The kid walked backward two jerky steps. He stared

at Clint in disbelief. Death was still in his eyes. He sat down abruptly, then flopped back limply and was still.

''Man enough,'' Clint murmured. Gun leveled, he looked at the crowd. To a man they shrank back from him.

A muffled cry sounded from the porch, and suddenly Elaine was dashing toward him. She caught him and hugged him with a frantic strength, half-sobbing as she did. Instinctively, Clint encircled her shoulders with his free arm.

He spotted Sledger standing alone near the edge of the crowd. Even from where he stood, he could discern the big man's glare. He reckoned he knew who had played a big hand in goading the kid to his death.

Gently, he disentangled himself from Elaine and thumbed shells from his belt to replace the two he'd fired. Then he went to look at the man he'd killed.

Chapter Six

Listlessly, Jason Rancon shuffled the tattered deck of cards on the table in front of him. He didn't bother to deal. He had lost too much of late in solitaire, and there were no odds in cheating yourself.

He eyed the shabby interior of the run-down bar and winced. Things had gone sour fast in this sorry backwater town, what with drunken cowboys still being sharp enough to spot how he dealt the cards, and Brandon and his enforcers getting upset when he had to defend himself.

He studied his hands as they shuffled the cards. A few years ago those cowpokes would never have spotted the tricks when he dealt. He was getting too old to make his way on the turn of a card, particularly if he wanted to control the turn.

A figure entered the saloon from the night outside, and Rancon smiled thinly. Maybe he was too old to deal the cards, but he would still show Brandon that he could play his hand well enough to win when the stakes were high. And these stakes were high enough so that he could think of giving up the life of aces and kings. Maybe he would go down to Mexico, bask in the sun like a lizard, drink tequila, and grow fat and lazy.

"You look mighty pleased with yourself," Quick Handley growled.

Rancon widened his grin a little bit as he directed it at the gunman. Handley was the card that had turned this town from a busted hand to a full house. "After tonight, we'll all have a right to look pleased with ourselves," Rancon replied.

Handley scowled and took a chair at the table. He still had his doubts about their scheme, Rancon knew, but he was over a barrel and couldn't get off. His choice had been made when, after Rancon had cleaned him out at the poker table, he had drunkenly boasted of knowing the whereabouts of a certain stolen gold shipment. From then on, it had been too late for him, because Carter Brandon wouldn't take kindly to news of one of his top hands spreading secrets about gold shipments that the fellow himself had helped steal on Brandon's orders.

Rancon had seen the value of the hold he had on Handley, and he had wasted no time in using it for his own benefit. The tricky part of blackmailing Handley had been to make sure that he didn't give the gun hand a chance to assure his silence with a bullet from his pearl-handled .45.

The other two owlhoots involved in the raid had

been killed by the men guarding the gold shipment. Brandon was unable to dispose of the gold until some of the dust settled, and he was holding it under guard right here in White City.

The odds were high, but this was a gamble Rancon hadn't been able to resist. If he was careful, he could manipulate Handley like a deck of marked cards, but Handley was a reluctant and potentially dangerous tool. Rancon had wanted another hole card to put the odds a little more in his favor. He hadn't had to look far.

"Where's Buck?" Handley demanded in a surly tone.

Rancon kept his grin in place. He knew it irritated people. "He'll meet up with us like we planned."

Handley's scowl deepened as he glanced anxiously about the dim interior of the saloon. They were alone but for the drunken barkeep.

"Rein it in," Rancon advised. "Brandon won't be back until we're a long way out on the trail."

"He didn't like me turning up with a bellyache and begging off on riding with him this time." Handley darted his fingers to touch the butt of his Colt. "I swear he suspected something."

Rancon shrugged. "Doesn't matter. He's still gone and we're holding all the high cards." He cut the deck neatly.

A distant shot sounded. Handley jerked convulsively about in his chair and grabbed for his gun.

Rancon let his lip curl slightly in disgust. Handley was behaving like a greenhorn, and he'd be glad to be rid of him once this was over. "You checked on the guard?" he asked to distract Handley from his fears.

"Yeah," Handley answered. "Nothing's changed. There's only one man."

"And he still doesn't know what he's guarding?"

Handley shook his head. "Only reason I knew about it was because I helped to steal it. I don't think Brandon's told anybody except maybe that ox, Sledger, and he's hanging around Brandon's house, like usual."

"What about Bradlock?"

"Naw, he don't know nothing about it. I told you, Brandon don't trust nobody except himself. He didn't want anybody to be tempted by that gold, including Bradlock."

Rancon remembered his brief exchange with the infamous gunslinger last night. "I hear he killed a man today."

Handley nodded jerkily. "Some fool kid looking for a rep. He picked the wrong hombre. Bradlock's fast as a greased rattler."

"Faster than you?" Rancon goaded.

Handley's eyes went real mean. "That ain't funny."

Rancon made a soothing gesture with his left hand. He was careful to leave his right close to his lapel and the revolver beneath it. He regretted the remark. Handley's greed and fear of Brandon had enabled Rancon to draw him into the fold, and it would be foolish to provoke him now. "Relax. I don't want to tangle with Bradlock, either. Did you spot him tonight?"

"Aw, he's prowling around like some durned lobo

wolf.'' Handley glanced sharply toward the door, as if he expected Brandon's *segundo* to be lurking just beyond in the darkness.

Rancon pulled forth his pocket watch and flipped open the scratched and dented cover. ''It's time to get moving.'' He squared the cards and dropped the deck into his vest pocket.

Handley hawked and spat onto the dirt floor. ''Ain't none too soon for me!''

Outside, the night air was hot and dry. Rancon smelled dust and garbage and alcohol on the sullen breeze. He hesitated and looked at Handley. ''The horses?''

''Out back.''

Handley disappeared into the gloom between the ramshackle buildings. Rancon followed him. Handley had tethered their mounts to a post at the rear of the saloon. They untied the animals and led them through the darkness behind the row of tents and structures lining that side of the main street. Rancon could hear odd scurryings and scramblings in the darkness around them. The stench of trash and offal was even stronger here. The muted sounds of voices and music filtered from the saloons and gambling dens they passed.

''Here it is,'' Handley whispered harshly.

Rancon saw that they had reached the rear of the Elephant Saloon. Its two-story height was distinctive.

''So where is he?'' Handley demanded.

A horse snorted in the gloom out beyond the buildings. Handley turned sharply, and even Rancon had to

still an impulsive grab for the short-barreled revolver
in his shoulder holster. A horseman loomed before
them.

"Evening, gents," a voice drawled.

Rancon could see that Buck Dilter was grinning as
if, despite the danger, he relished what they were about
to do. The lean gun hawk's resentment over Carter
Brandon's high-handed dismissal of him had burned
deep, and he had been easy to recruit for this job. The
idea of getting rich at Brandon's expense appealed to
him mightily.

Dilter dismounted and nodded to them both in greeting. "Are we ready?" he asked with hard eagerness.

"We're ready," Rancon assured him. "Take the
horses."

Dilter loosened his pistol in his holster, then took
the reins of their horses.

"Keep your eyes peeled," Rancon told him. "Sing
out if there's any trouble you can't handle, and don't
use that gun if you can help it. We want to ride out of
here with nobody the wiser."

"Yeah, yeah. We've gone over all this afore now.
Let's get it done."

Rancon reckoned that Dilter would play out his hand
to the end. He turned to Handley. "Come on."

Treading carefully to avoid the debris in the alley,
Rancon crossed to the warped door in the building's
unpainted board wall. With his right hand near the lapel
of his coat, he used his left one to grasp the knob and
turn it.

As expected, the door was unlocked. The Elephant was a saloon, not a bank, even if Brandon was using a part of it like one. A dim and dusty hallway lined with doors was before him. Behind the doors, he knew, were the cribs where drunks slept off their excesses.

Only one door was different. In front of it, a bored gun hand lounged in a chair tilted back against the wall. As the rear door opened, he rocked the chair forward to the floor and turned curious eyes toward them.

Rancon let himself be seen. He kept his hands in plain sight now. "Mind if we come in this way?" he inquired agreeably.

The guard rose to his feet. "I reckon not." He was eyeing Rancon warily. Rancon wished he had remained seated, but his reputation as a troublemaker in White City was probably known to the fellow. Then the guard relaxed slightly as he recognized Quick Handley behind Rancon.

"Any trouble back here?" Handley asked over Rancon's shoulder as they drew near.

The guard shook his head. "Real quiet tonight." A trace of puzzlement was in his tone.

They had drawn abreast of him now with Rancon in the lead. Rancon paused and turned as if to speak. The guard's eyes were on him, not Handley, his fellow enforcer. Rancon grinned wickedly. The guard blinked in surprise. Then he grunted as, unseen, Handley thrust the knife between his ribs with a single lightning movement of his arm. Deftly, Rancon plucked the gun from his holster before the guard's stricken hand could close on it. He stepped back to let him collapse into his chair.

Cursing softly, Handley wiped his blade clean on the dead man's shirt. Rancon glanced up and down the hall. There had been no alarm. From the front of the saloon, the muffled sounds of revelry continued unabated.

Handley spat out another oath as he sheathed his knife. "I hated to do that," he said bitterly. "I knew him. Drank with him once."

"No choice," Rancon reminded him. "We couldn't leave him alive to put Brandon on our trail."

"I know, blast it! Get the door open, will you?"

Rancon tried the knob. Unlike the doors of the drunk cribs, it had a lock, but a flimsy one. He stepped back and kicked hard. On the second impact of his heel, wood splintered and the door swung inward.

"Come on. Get him inside," Rancon ordered.

Together they hauled the guard's body out of the hallway. Rancon fumbled to light a lamp before heeling the broken door shut behind them. In the pale flickering light he saw a chair and desk. A file cabinet was against the wall. Beside it was a metal strongbox.

"Full house!" Rancon exulted aloud.

He crossed swiftly to the box and dropped to one knee. He was careful to keep Handley in his side vision. The gun hand was alternating eager glances at the box with fearful ones toward the door.

There was a padlock, Rancon saw. Doubtless Brandon would have replaced the original one. The gun boss probably carried the key on his person. Rancon tested the weight of the box. It was the gold for certain. Nothing else would be that heavy.

"Let's get it outside," he ordered. He would have liked to riffle the desk and the file cabinet, but the longer they stayed, the worse the odds got.

They lugged the box out of the room. Rancon extinguished the lamp and pulled the door shut as they left. With any luck it would be some time before the guard's body was found, maybe not even until Brandon himself returned.

With the box between them, they shuffled back the way they had come. They were almost at the hallway's end when a door opened behind them.

Even hampered by the handle of the box in his left hand, Handley got his gun out fast. He twisted about, extending it at arm's length. Rancon saw a drunken cowpoke just lurching out of one of the cribs. He staggered down the hall away from them. Heading back to the saloon, he didn't look behind him.

Handley lowered his gun but didn't reholster it. Sweat gleamed on his face. Rancon could feel it on his own as well. They hefted the box out the door.

Dilter came forward, tugging impatiently on the reins of the horses. He eyed the strongbox hungrily. "Blamed if you didn't get it!" He chuckled harshly.

"Set it down." Rancon pulled his revolver from under his coat. Inside, he hadn't wanted to risk a shot, but here he felt safer. Besides, he didn't plan to ride out without knowing for sure what he had.

He thrust the gun barrel down close to the padlock, turned his face aside, and pulled the trigger. The blast sounded like a cannon going off. The shattered padlock spun away. Rancon blinked at the powder smoke that stung his eyes. Handley brushed past him to fling back the lid.

Peering down at the box's contents, Dilter breathed a curse of satisfaction. Even in the gloom of the alley, the neatly stacked ingots seemed to glow with a yellow light of their own. Rancon felt a surge of triumph. He had gambled big, and now he was raking in his winnings.

"Let's ride out of here," he said hoarsely.

"Does anybody know who did this?" Clint raised his voice to be heard over the murmur of the voices of the men clustered in the hallway outside the shabby office.

There were only mumbled or profane negatives in answer to his query. He stared bleakly down at the sprawled body for a moment, then looked back at the spectators. A few bar girls had joined them and were peering into the room with wide eyes. Even in White City, murder like this was a little out of the ordinary. He vaguely remembered the dead man's name as Mitch. He had been one of Brandon's enforcers.

"Anybody see anything?" he tried again.

Apparently nobody had. The killing wasn't more

than a couple of hours old, he guessed. A drunken patron of the Elephant had literally stumbled over the body while looking for a spot to bed down. The sight had sobered him enough to make him start hollering for help. But the help hadn't come soon enough for Mitch.

''What is this place?'' Clint jerked his head to indicate the room.

''Boss uses it as some kind of office,'' one of the enforcers spoke up. ''Never let nobody in. Always had a guard posted.''

Brandon hadn't told Clint about whatever secrets the room had housed. Clint wondered if the murder had been nothing more than a petty thief's scheme to pilfer Brandon's office that had gone murderously awry. There were no signs that the killer had taken anything, and no way of knowing for sure until Brandon returned.

He looked again at the corpse. The knife meant that the killer had been close, and it might also mean that Mitch had known his murderer well enough not to mistrust him until it was too late.

Clint frowned. ''Bob, Al, roust out the drunks in the cribs and ask if any of them saw anything,'' he commanded. ''Pete, you round up a few more boys and ask around in the saloon. If you don't learn anything, start checking the other places in town.''

The three gunmen hurried away to follow his orders. Clint shouldered his way through the curious saloon patrons and bar girls. He plucked a lantern from a peg on the wall and headed down the hall toward the rear door. It wasn't too likely that a sneak thief with his victim's blood still on his hands would pass boldly out through the saloon to make his escape.

A few of the onlookers followed Clint. He ignored them. In the alley he halted and extended the lantern in front of him. For a moment he studied the ground in the wavering light. The alley was cluttered with trash and debris, but he was an old hand at reading sign in worse conditions than these. More than once his life had ridden on his skill.

He took a pair of careful steps forward, then dropped onto his haunches. He held the lantern a few inches above the ground. Traffic would have been light back here since the crime, he figured. Only vaguely was he conscious of the bar patrons watching him curiously.

The marks were faint on the hard ground. He would have to wait until daylight to be certain, but he was willing to bet that three men had been involved in the crime. And that they had taken something from the office—some sort of strongbox, from the looks of the impressions. Raising the lantern a little higher, he spotted a shattered padlock nearby.

He rose to his feet. He was willing to bet, too, on the identities of the three robbers and the loot they had taken away with them. Rancon and his owlhoots must have been making their plans when he had observed them the night before. It was likely that the missing gold shipment of Howard Herns was no longer in White City.

Something white caught his eye and he stooped to

pick it up. He was holding a small rectangle of pasteboard. He wondered how long it would be before Rancon realized that he'd lost an ace.

"You were supposed to look after things here!" Brandon roared. His handsome face was dark with fury as he stalked his office.

Clint shifted slightly in the guard's chair that he had pulled into the small room. "You never told me there was anything to look after back here in these cribs." He put a slight edge on his voice.

"My mistake!" Brandon snapped. He worked the fingers of his hand above the holstered butt of his fancy pistol.

"What did they take?" Clint asked mildly.

Brandon swung his head sharply toward him, then appeared to relax slightly. "Gold," he said tightly. "A lot of it."

Clint raised an eyebrow. "You keep lots of gold stored around here, do you?"

"There were problems with this gold. The way I got it made some important people mad." Brandon's smile was a grin of satisfaction. Then rage suffused his face again. "Do you know who did it?"

Clint slipped the playing card from under his gun belt and held it between his fingertips for Brandon to see.

"So?" Brandon spat.

"Rancon. I did some checking. Word is, he was seen with Handley and Buck Dilter two nights ago, and now neither Rancon nor Handley are anywhere to be found.''

Brandon cursed explosively. ''I should have killed Buck in the first place! And I thought it was awful peculiar how Handley came down with a bellyache the way he did.''

''It just happened last night,'' Clint prodded a little. ''We can still go after them.''

He'd had the notion last night that it was smarter to stay close to Brandon than to ride out on a manhunt to recover the gold, even if he could be certain that Rancon and his cohorts had it. Since he knew for sure now that it was the gold shipment that had been stolen, maybe he could do both.

Brandon had ridden back into town late that afternoon. His mood was already murderous. ''I had problems!'' he had growled in reply to Clint's query about his early return. He was two men short, Clint noted.

''Yeah, we'll go after them at first light,'' Brandon vowed now.

''I'll collect some of the men,'' Clint said, rising.

Brandon waved him back. ''No,'' he brooded aloud. ''This has turned personal. I got a score to settle with Buck and Handley, and I can't afford to let the rest of the men see me buffaloed by two skunks like that. Riding them down with an army wouldn't mean a blamed thing. No, we'll go after them all right, but it'll be us, just you and me. We'll track them down and bring the gold back ourselves!''

Chapter Seven

Clint saw Elaine watching them from her porch when they rode out at daybreak. She waved hesitantly in farewell, whether to him or Brandon he didn't know. Brandon ignored her. Clint figured it best to do likewise.

He spotted Sledger filling the doorway of the small shed where he bunked. The big prizefighter seemed to be gazing at Elaine's solitary figure in front of the big house.

Clint could still feel the soft warmth of her as she had held him after the gunfight. The memories of her touch and of their afternoon together stirred things in his spirit that he'd thought were dead and buried. What did the Good Book say about a virtuous woman? She was worth far more than rubies. Well, he reckoned he'd found a virtuous woman. But even if the fences between them weren't well nigh impossible to jump, what could she possibly see in the cold soul and cynical conscience of a man who lived by the gun?

He cut his eyes over to Brandon, who was sitting a

powerful black gelding. His second horse, a rangy bay, trailed behind at the end of a lead rope. The gun boss reminded Clint of a hawk circling to spot his prey. He figured that Brandon wouldn't be too happy to know that his *segundo*'s thoughts occupied themselves with his lovely young ward.

Clint's own spare horse was a long-legged sorrel. By switching their horses, Clint knew, they could go a lot faster than men on single mounts. Brandon had suggested the tactic, that of a man experienced in hunting human prey. Clint recollected Elaine's comment that her guardian had once served as some kind of range detective. What else had Brandon done in his checkered past?

Clint had donned his drab tracker's clothes and high Apache moccasins. Brandon wore his usual range attire. They had picked up the trail behind the Elephant Saloon. The tracks were easy enough to follow in the daylight. Rancon and his accomplices hadn't been trying to cover their trail, just to put some distance between themselves and their crime.

"I figure they probably rode through the night and the next day before stopping," Brandon said as they rode. "Means their horses will be worn down some, even with a night's rest. They're likely taking it easier today, since there hasn't been any sign of a chase." He gave Clint a dark look as he spoke the last.

Clint ignored the look. "Could be they split up."

Brandon shook his head. "Those sidewinders won't trust each other enough to divide up the gold until they're sure they've ridden clear of trouble. Each of them will think the others might double back and try for all the gold.''

The reasoning was good enough, Clint decided. ''You sound like you've done this sort of thing before,'' he commented casually.

''Shoot, I've done *everything* before,'' Brandon said grimly.

''Riders coming.''

Brandon followed the direction of his gaze and grunted as he saw the pair of horsemen cresting a hill about a quarter mile distant. ''Let's check if they've seen anything.'' He reined his black toward them.

The pair of strangers pulled in their horses and waited uncertainly. They were headed in the general direction of White City and appeared to be cowpokes slicked up for a time on the town. Clint guessed that they had gotten their wages and ridden all night to reach their sinful goal.

''Howdy, fellows,'' Brandon greeted them affably enough as they drew up to the pair. ''Where you headed?''

One cowpoke was a few years older than the other. They exchanged sidelong glances, as if a little spooked by what they saw in the hard men before them. ''Fixing to go to Beer City,'' the older man said as he grinned a bit nervously.

''Is that a fact?'' Brandon responded. ''Where you from?''

''Trail herd.'' The spokesman jerked his head over

his shoulder. "There'll be some more of us along here shortly. Ned and me just got a jump on them other fellows."

"You boys seen hide or hair of three hombres riding kind of fast? One's a tinhorn gambler and the others ain't no strangers to guns." Brandon's tone had shed some of its affability.

Both cowboys shook their heads. Again it was the older one who answered: "No sirree. Haven't seen nobody since we left the herd last night."

Brandon mulled it over for a moment, then nodded as if satisfied. The two cowhands relaxed visibly. "You're talking to Carter Brandon," the gun boss went on more agreeably. "I run things over at Beer City. This here's Clint Bradlock. He sides me."

Clint saw the eyes of the two men widen in recognition. Brandon seemed to be enjoying the evil notoriety of their names, he noted somberly.

"It's a great pleasure to meet you!" the younger cowpoke spoke up for the first time, and in awe.

The older man's horse shifted as if he were suddenly eager to be away. "We'll sure keep our eyes peeled for those jaspers you described," he vowed.

"They're long gone," Brandon told him. "But thanks just the same. When you hit Beer City, go to the Elephant Saloon. Can't miss it. Biggest place in town. Once you've been there, you can say you've seen the elephant! Tell the bartender that Carter Brandon said to be sure you got your money's worth!"

"Yessir, Mr. Brandon!" the youngster cried eagerly. His partner nodded in parting and prodded his cow pony with his spurs.

"Did you see that gun Brandon was packing?" Clint heard the youngster say as the two galloped off. "I ain't never seen nothing like that!" Clint couldn't hear his partner's reply.

Brandon gazed after them. "They'll leave White City broke as puppy dogs," he said with satisfaction. Then he looked in the direction that he and Clint had been traveling. "They hadn't seen anything, so Rancon and his skunks probably haven't doubled back. Means they've got no place to go. There's nothing much up ahead except a whole lot of prairie."

Clint glanced back once as they rode on, but the cowpokes were no longer in sight.

Brandon noticed his caution. "Checking the back-trail," he observed aloud in a caustic tone.

"A man lives longer that way."

"You killed some fellow in town yesterday, didn't you?"

Clint frowned. "He wasn't much more than a kid."

"If he's old enough to pack a gun and pull it on you, then he's a man."

"Yeah," Clint agreed tiredly. "But he won't be pulling on nobody else."

As Brandon had said, the trail of their quarry led them on across the undulating grassland. They rode at the best pace they could manage while not losing the trail. Signs of the horses' passage in the tall buffalo grass were usually pretty plain, but more than once they were forced to halt and check patches of barren ground for elusive hoofprints.

True to his boast, Brandon was no greenhorn at tracking, and Clint had the unnerving thought that the gun boss wouldn't be a bad choice of a partner to ride the bounty trail. What did that say about himself and the kind of man he had become? Clint queried his conscience, but the muffled drum of horse hooves on the grass was the only answer he got.

With the sun nigh to being straight overhead, they halted below the summit of a hill to switch horses. Both the gelding and the paint were holding up well enough, but there was no gain in testing their limits. Clint uncinched his saddle and hefted it onto the back of the fresh sorrel.

"I'll be hanged!" Brandon exclaimed softly. "Would you look at that?"

Clint shifted his gaze to where he indicated. A couple of hundred yards distant, three massive brown shapes were lumbering into the shelter of a rocky draw.

"Buffalo!" he said aloud, and heard the surprise in his own voice.

"Didn't think there were any of them left running free," Brandon said, still staring at the distant animals.

For just a moment one of the beasts—a massive old bull—swung his head in their direction. Sunlight glinted off the curving horns on either side of his broad brow. The breeze must have carried their scent and spooked the beasts.

The old bull vanished from sight in the draw. Clint

felt as though he'd just seen a ghost out of the prairie's past. Like gunfighters, the buffalo were a vanishing breed. But a few small and isolated groups must still exist out on these trackless plains. He guessed that the mass slaughter of the herds over the past several decades had forced these remnants to a life of concealment and solitude, driving them to take to cover whenever men came near. He wondered how much longer the noble creatures could survive.

Brandon reached for his Winchester in its saddle sheath. ''The head and hide of one of those critters would fetch a good price these days,'' he said with tight eagerness.

''Are we out here to hunt buffalo or to track down Rancon and your gold?'' Clint asked.

Brandon hesitated, then shoved the rifle back. ''You're right,'' he conceded with ill grace. He shook his head and cast a last regretful look at the spot where the animals had disappeared. ''Buffalo. Who would have believed it?''

The sorrel and the bay seemed glad to be in the lead. Clint chewed on a strip of jerky and washed it down with a sip from his canteen as they rode. Brandon looked content with an occasional pull from his pocket flask. They had brought supplies for several days, but only a tenderfoot ate more than necessary when riding an uncertain trail.

In the distance, gray and purple clouds built up, and a summer rainstorm rushed across the grasslands. White spears of lightning stabbed at the ground in the blink of an eye. Thunder rumbled hollowly far off. In eerie contrast, the sun still shone brightly where they rode.

With the fading storm far to their backs, Brandon pulled up on his reins and squinted at the ground. "Their horses are plumb near tuckered out," he concluded after a moment. "We ain't far behind them now."

Clint looked ahead to where the island shapes of a series of rugged rocky hills jutted up from the grass. "Could be they've holed up in those hills," he said. "We'd best take care about skylining ourselves."

Before Brandon could reply, a rifle shot plucked the hat neatly from his head.

Elaine lifted her fingers from the piano keys and let the last notes die into the silence of the parlor. Despite her best efforts, even the gay tunes had a melancholy tone today. Her fingers—or perhaps her heart—would not be governed by the dictates of her mind.

And what had brought about this sadness of her spirit? she wondered. The loneliness of her sequestered existence here was nothing new to her. She had learned to endure it over the months since she had obeyed her guardian's instructions to come here. She had her piano, her Bible, and her books to fend off the solitude. So what had made today so different?

In her mind's eye flashed the handsome face of Clint Bradlock, and in her heart she knew that here was the source of her sadness. The afternoon spent with him had been like awakening from a gloomy dream to find a bright morning filled with sunshine and the promise of a joyous future. She longed to be near him again. His absence only accentuated her loneliness.

She was being foolish, she chided herself. And such thoughts were surely improper. But they persisted nonetheless, as did the appealing image of Clint Bradlock.

She knew he was a gunman of infamous reputation in the Territory. She had overheard Carter and Sledger discussing him once. Most gunmen were nothing more than hired killers, but somehow she couldn't reconcile the strong compassionate man she was coming to know with a cold-blooded killer. He had tried to avoid the gunfight in which he had killed the young man who had drawn on him. Afterward, he had been severely stricken by what he had been forced to do. In his eyes, she had read a loneliness to match her own. She felt a faint heat rising to her face as she recalled the impulsive way she had hugged him in sheer relief over his safety.

Still, she cautioned herself, there was the fact that he was working for her uncle as a kind of hired gun. But she was sure in her heart that he was different from the other hard-eyed men working for Carter.

If so, why was he doing it? Troubled, she rose from the piano and took a slow, aimless turn about the parlor. She caught a glimpse of herself in a large oval mirror and paused unthinkingly to study her appearance. She ran her hands down her modest white dress to smooth out the wrinkles, and straightened the white ribbon set in her black hair.

She realized abruptly that she was imagining how Clint would see her, and she turned away from the mirror with a swirl of her dress.

Resolutely, she moved to the chaise longue by the window and seated herself. She reached for a book of poetry, but found her eyes drawn out the window to the grassland rolling away into the distance. From this vantage point she could not see any of the rest of the town at all. It was as if the ugliness of White City did not exist.

She had ridden across that grassland with Clint yesterday, treasuring his smile, his rare laughter. And she had watched him and Carter ride out that morning on the trail of the robbers. Where were they now? she wondered. What were they doing? Were they in danger? She shivered and offered up a silent prayer for their safety.

Clint was like her uncle in some ways, she reflected. Both of them were strong, capable men who had seen the world and knew how to take care of themselves in it. But in so many indefinable and subtle ways, Clint was different from Carter Brandon. Perhaps they were ways that only a woman could see.

She recollected her father's saying that Carter had always had a wild streak. As a child she had thought Carter a gallant and heroic figure with his adventurous tales of outlaws and range wars. But there was a ruthlessness to him now that she had never detected as a hero-worshiping child.

And there was something more, she admitted to herself with a shrinking of her spirit. She had not acknowledged it to anyone else, not even to Clint. She had first seen it in Carter's eyes when he showed up at her father's funeral. And though she sought to deny it, she had watched it burn more fiercely during her time here in White City.

Carter Brandon didn't look at her as a child anymore. Nor did he look at her as a ward or a niece or a daughter. In his hungry eyes she had become a woman, and she dared not face the full ramifications of what that might mean to her, held, as she was, a virtual prisoner in this fine house.

"Miss Elaine want lemonade?"

Elaine jumped in surprise. "Oh, Vieja. You scared me!" The old woman had appeared before her like part of a conjurer's act. "Yes, please, some lemonade would be nice," she recovered enough to reply.

Oddly, Vieja hesitated. "Your mind sees the young warrior," she said.

"Young warrior?" Elaine echoed in puzzlement.

Vieja made a little nodding motion with her head, but didn't speak.

"Oh, you mean Clint—Mr. Bradlock," Elaine said in understanding.

Vieja grunted expressively. Her wise eyes were black as polished onyx. "He good man," she announced with emphasis.

A surge of affection for the old woman rose up in Elaine. "I think so too, Vieja!" she exclaimed softly.

"He make good brave. He take good care of his woman," Vieja went on.

"But I didn't mean—" Elaine broke off. What did she mean?

Unexpectedly, Vieja smiled like a schoolgirl sharing secrets with her friends. Cackling gleefully, she turned and shuffled from the room. Elaine stared after her in bemusement. She knew that if she looked in the mirror, she would be blushing furiously.

She forced herself to pick up her book and open it, but her eyes would not focus on the printed words.

She heard the front door open suddenly, and looked up in surprise. Heavy footsteps sounded, and the next instant Sledger was looming in the doorway to the parlor. Elaine stifled a gasp. He seemed to fill the space between the doorjambs. His thick lips were open in what was almost a grin. He still carried the bruises of his recent prizefight.

Elaine fought the wild urge to scramble to her feet. Instead, she rose from the chaise as casually as possible. She realized she was gripping her book tightly in both hands. She had never known Sledger to set foot in the house without Carter's being present, and certainly never without permission.

"What do you want?" Her voice came out at a higher pitch than she'd intended.

"Just checking to make sure you're all right," he answered in his rough voice. "Can't be too careful after them fellows busted in the other night. Could be, they're still hanging around.''

"I'm fine, thank you." Her voice was firmer now. "Please leave."

Her words didn't seem to reach him. He turned his head, topped with its absurd stocking cap, and looked slowly about the room. As his eyes came back to her, he lifted a blunt thumb and scratched at his nose. "Mighty pretty place Mr. Brandon fixed up for you here. 'Course, you're a mighty pretty woman." His lips widened in an expression that was far more awful than a grin. "Been meaning to tell you that for a long time."

Elaine's heart battered at her ribs. "Please leave," she repeated as firmly as she could. "Uncle Carter won't be happy that you were here."

"*Uncle.*" Sledger gave a derisive snort of laughter. Then he sobered. "You know, I've been real polite and proper with you for a long time now. Always a gentleman. Figured that earned me a little respect or something from you." A scowl began to darken his heavy brow. "But you never paid no attention to me. Then I see you hugging all over that sorry gun hawk Bradlock like some kind of saloon floozy. I figure if he's good enough for you, then so am I."

"Get out," Elaine ordered.

Instead, he took a step farther into the room. "Uh-uh. Not till I've had my say. Mr. Brandon don't ever need to know about me coming to visit you. And I think I'll be doing that right frequently from here on."

"Carter will kill you," she warned desperately.

Rage and what might have been fear made his brutish features even uglier. "I reckon you better not tell him unless you want to see that pretty face of yours ruined." He lifted a clenched fist that was almost as large as her head.

She was at his mercy, she thought in horror. No man in White City would stand up to him in Carter's absence. She knew without doubt that Clint Bradlock would defend her honor if he were here, but he was gone with her uncle. Frantically, she cast her eyes about for a weapon.

Her terror must have shown in her face. Sledger chuckled like a ghoul. "You just do some thinking on it, honey," he advised with a lewd grin. "I ain't so bad once you get to know me. Leastways, being friendly to me is a sight better than having that pretty face all beat up." He leered a moment longer, then turned and lumbered out of the room.

When she heard the front door close behind him, she allowed her knees to weaken. Sagging, she held the back of the chaise to keep from falling. Movement caught the side of her vision. Vieja had appeared in the room beside her. Elaine saw a brief glint of metal, as if the old woman was concealing something in her buckskin dress. Then Vieja's strong hands were supporting her.

"Evil man!" Vieja spat.

Elaine understood that the old woman had overheard

everything said by Sledger. "Vieja," she moaned, "what am I going to do?"

Murmuring wordlessly, Vieja drew her to her breast. Held in her comforting arms, Elaine closed her tearful eyes and prayed.

Chapter Eight

"They're up there, sure enough."
Brandon's tone was fierce.
From where he lay on a grassy crest, he sighted down the barrel of his Winchester and fired.

He was shooting blind, Clint thought, but it might serve to discourage the bushwhackers. He himself was on his belly a little distant from Brandon. With his rifle beside him, he used field glasses to search the high, rocky hill from which the shots had come.

Their horses were at the foot of the hill. So far only one man had thrown lead at them.

"Could be the other two are running away on the far side of that hill," Clint suggested.

Brandon shook his head. "They ain't running no more!"

Clint tended to think he was right. Their quarry had good cover, and they knew now that only two pursuers were after them. In order to reach the rugged hill, a man would have to cross a good quarter mile of open country under a hostile gun. Here, there was no way

111

to creep up on the dry-gulcher as he had stalked the lone guard back in the Wichita Mountains.

"That hombre shooting at us must be their lookout," Clint said. "All three of them will be joining in with him before much longer. Come nightfall, no telling what they'll do."

Brandon grunted a wordless assent. Carefully, he reached back and extracted his flask from his hip pocket. He unscrewed the cap and threw down a gulp. Clint caught the scent of the whiskey.

Sunlight glinted suddenly off metal on the rocky face of the hill.

"There!" Brandon said with savage satisfaction. "Did you see it?"

"I saw it."

Brandon slid the flash into his pocket and began to wriggle backward down the hill. "Keep him pinned down," he commanded. "When I get over there, I'll cover you."

As he spoke, he was rising into a crouch, taking care not to skyline himself. He was still without his hat, and moved swiftly down the slope to the horses. Clint levered his Winchester and put a shot where he had seen the distant reflection. He waited a few seconds and then fired again, this time a little to one side of the same spot.

A wild rebel yell sounded from below him, and an instant later Brandon's black gelding and bay burst into sight. As they raced toward the hill, Clint saw Brandon clinging between them like an Indian warrior of old.

It was as fancy a bit of riding as he'd ever seen, and it was straight into the barrel of an enemy gun.

Clint fired and fired again, punching bullets as fast as he could at the opposite hillside. He was dimly aware of another rifle opening up from over there. One of the other two thieves had added his gun to the issue.

Before Clint could draw a bead on the new rifleman, he saw Brandon's bay stumble and fall away from the black. One of the enemy bullets had found a target. But the black raced on with Brandon clinging to its side like a burr. Clint's rifle ran dry. At the same moment Brandon reached the base of the hill and flung himself from the gelding to the shelter of a jumble of boulders.

Clint didn't quite believe the feat he'd just seen. Automatically he began to jam shells into the Winchester as he scanned the boulders where Brandon had taken cover. Had the gun boss really missed catching a bullet in his daredevil ride?

The outlaws' rifles had fallen silent. The steepness of the hill might be keeping them from having a clear shot down at Brandon's new position. Movement caught Clint's eye among the boulders. An upraised arm motioned for him to come ahead. Brandon was ready to cover him.

Clint snaked backward from the crest of the rise. Once on his feet, he descended the remaining yards to the paint and the sorrel, and then he switched his saddle back to the paint. The animal was a favorite mount of his and knew him well while the sorrel was one of

Brandon's string. Having familiar horseflesh under him might make a heap of difference in surviving what awaited him. There would be at least two rifles aiming at him, and he wasn't sure how effective Brandon's cover fire would be from his sheltered position.

But Clint didn't have much in the way of options. He couldn't leave Brandon over there to face the killers alone on hostile terrain.

Astride the paint, he caught the sorrel's lead rope, shifted the paint's reins to his teeth, and drew the Winchester from its scabbard with his left hand. The reins tasted of salt in his mouth. He braced the rifle's butt against the saddle and swung his head from side to side to test the reins. The paint responded well enough to the awkward means of control.

Clint worked his teeth more firmly into the leather. He had no intention of trying to imitate Brandon's stunt and didn't even think he could manage it. But he had a few tricks of his own. He hoped grimly that they would be enough to keep him alive.

He guided the paint around the side of the hill, keeping the sorrel on a short lead. Ready, he dropped the sorrel's rope, filled his right hand with his .45, and snapped a shot just above the sorrel's head. The startled animal broke from the cover of the slope and bolted into the open. Clint put heels hard to the paint and took off in the sorrel's wake.

The spooked sorrel was streaking away at a dead run. For those first instants, the outlaws' eyes and guns would be on the sorrel. He had that much leeway, and he drove the paint for all the beast was worth.

As the wind tore at his face, he sawed his head from side to side, sending the paint forward in a zigzagging charge. Right and left, with Colt and rifle, he cut loose at the hill. He thumbed the Colt's hammer and pulled the trigger as fast as he could. He thrust the rifle out at arm's length and fired, letting the recoil flip his arm up, and using the motion to work the lever and snap the gun back down to fire again. He knew he didn't have a hope of hitting anything except maybe the hill itself, but the barrage of fire out of his wild charge might make the outlaws keep their heads down.

Faintly, he fancied that he heard the rapid-fire stutter of Brandon's fancy pistol. He had lost track of the sorrel, and he wondered if it had been hit by a stray bullet. A bullwhip seemed to pop next to his ear. A shot had come within inches of him. Desperately, he jigged the paint aside. At least one of the owlhoots had found his range.

Then the rock-studded hill was looming above him. The gunfire dwindled. One last shot sent a bullet screaming off in a ricochet. He had no idea how close it had come. He piled off the paint and dashed to the shelter of the boulders. Brandon was shoving a new magazine into the butt of his pistol. He rammed it home with the heel of his hand.

Clint realized his legs were shaking. His breath was coming in ragged gasps. He spat to clear the taste of salt from his mouth, and slumped against a towering boulder. He began to fumble for shells to his six-gun. He had shot it dry.

"Took your time," Brandon said sardonically. He was breathing a little hard himself.

Clint spared him a glance. "I hear they're looking for good trick riders in the Wild West shows these days. You could give the folks back East a real thrill."

Brandon snorted. "They're looking for fancy two-gun shooters too. 'Course, you have to be able to hit something."

A bullet bounced off rock somewhere nearby. Clint cocked his head and gazed up at the rocky heights above them. "They're trying to get into position for a clear shot."

"Yeah. I still make it just two of them. Where do you reckon the other one is?"

"Don't know. Maybe covering the backside of the hill."

"How you want to work it?" Brandon's wide-set eyes were gauging him.

As he studied the slope, Clint caught a flicker of movement among the scrub brush and rocks. Another shot sounded. The bullet was closer this time. A cloud of powder smoke drifted up from a different point.

"There and there." Clint nodded at each spot. He had no doubt that Brandon had picked them out as well. "One of us lays down some cover fire while the other goes up after that jasper." He indicated the drifting powder smoke. It was the closer of the two points.

"You want to flip a coin?" Brandon asked dryly.

Clint shook his head. "Rancon's the gambling man. I ain't. At least, not on the flip of a coin. I'll gamble on you not hitting me with that foreign gun while I'm climbing."

Brandon's shrewd eyes never left him. "By rights, that ought to be my job. You're dealing yourself into my fight like it was your own."

Clint shifted his shoulders. "I'm getting paid to side you. Anyway, they're shooting at me too."

There was iron courage in Brandon, Clint reflected, and he felt a grudging kinship with the man. He wasn't eager to go up the hill after the bushwhackers, but down in his gut he didn't want to be responsible for keeping Brandon alive if he insisted on making the climb.

After a moment Brandon shrugged. "Suit yourself. I've got to admit you're earning your percentage of the take."

"Just keep those hombres pinned down."

Clint checked his bowie knife and his Colt, then hefted his Winchester in his left hand. He reloaded the rifle and placed his Stetson on a convenient rock. He lifted his head to study the rugged vastness above him. Two shots chipped rock nearby. Clint glanced at Brandon. The gun boss had his rifle in both hands, ready to snap it to his shoulder to fire. His pistol was holstered at his hip. He gave Clint a short go-ahead nod.

Clint eased out of the natural rocky fortress and went to ground on the slope. Belly to the earth, he started to work his way upward, slipping from one piece of cover to the next. There were plenty of rocks and shrubs to offer concealment. Behind him, Brandon's rifle began to respond to those of the outlaws.

Clint angled wide. He wanted to approach his quarry from the side or rear rather than right into the barrel of a rifle. He could feel the afternoon sun on his back and could smell the gritty earth and his own sweat as he inched and writhed his way upward.

He paused in a shallow defile to get his bearings. As the brush beside his face rustled, a scaly, triangular head poked into view, and then a black forked tongue tested the air of a foot in front of his staring eyes. He recognized the distinctive diamond markings of a rattler, a big one.

The snake paused. Clint held even his eyes motionless. From what he could see of the reptile, its body was nearly as thick as his arm. He wondered if he was fast enough to intercept it if it lashed out at him.

At last it began to move. He watched the thick body pass in front of him. It seemed an eternity before its rattles finally disappeared from view. The snake had been longer than his own body. He blinked his frozen eyes and tried to still the pounding of his heart.

Moving somewhat like the snake, he went on. No shots had been directed at him, which meant that the two bushwhackers must still think he was holed up below with Brandon. Where was the third man? He had no time to dwell on the question. At any moment the present two might realize that Brandon was alone.

Finally, in the shelter of a jagged outcropping of

stone, he rose cautiously into a crouch and peered around the edge of the outcropping. His calculations had been good. In front and a little below him, a rifleman was kneeling in the cover of a barren gully that angled down across the face of the hill. Clint saw that it was Quick Handley, the gunfighter who had replaced Buck. As he watched, Handley sighted and fired once more.

Clint looked past him along the face of the hill. The other sharpshooter was beyond him somewhere, maybe in his earlier position. Clint had lost track of the distorted echoes of gunfire during his climb.

He took a moment to chew things over. From his vantage point, he could drop Handley with an easy shot, but that might reveal his presence in their midst to the other outlaws. Could he take Handley silently with his knife?

Throwing a knife, particularly a bowie, was an uncertain maneuver at best, and he risked losing the knife. The terrain sloped sharply down to the gully. There was no cover. He'd be crossing twenty feet of steep, open ground to close with a man whose nerves would already be strung taut by the gun battle.

Clint laid his rifle at his feet and drew the bowie. Handley's ears were probably ringing like bells from the gunfire, and it might give Clint the edge he needed.

Like a cougar stalking a deer, he eased out of cover and went down the slope with short, silent steps. His Apache moccasins were soundless on the hard ground. He held the bowie low at his side.

He had covered three yards when Handley's rifle clicked empty. Handley shifted back from his kneeling position and felt in his clothes for shells. As he did so, his head turned slightly so that Clint was in his range of vision.

A curse exploded from Handley's lips, and he grabbed for his pearl-handled Colt. His hand was as fast as his name. Clint launched himself down into the gully. Handley's gun came out as he swiveled to bring it to bear. Clint crashed into him. He batted the gun arm aside and slammed the bowie home with all the momentum of his downward lunge. Handley's long-barreled Colt dropped unfired. Clint crouched over him, knife bared.

After a moment he drew back. As with the kid in White City, there had been no choice in the killing. His eye fell on a sheathed knife at the dead man's belt. If Handley had been the one who stabbed the guard, there would be a rough justice to his death.

Clint slipped from the gully and climbed up the slope to retrieve his Winchester. As he knelt to grasp it, he realized that the shooting had stopped. Had Brandon picked off the other sharpshooter, or had he, instead, fallen victim to the outlaw's gun? Clint could see nothing of either man.

Warily he crept to a higher point of vantage. Shading his eyes, he surveyed the terrain below him. He longed for his field glasses, but he had left them with his horse at the base of the hill. When movement flickered in a tangled thicket, he felt his muscles go tense. Squinting, he waited. In another moment he spotted his prey.

Rancon was moving pretty fast for a tinhorn gambler, Clint acknowledged. The varmint emerged from the thicket in a low, stalking stance thirty feet downslope, rifle at ready. He must suspect that something had happened to Handley, Clint figured, and was prowling closer to investigate.

Gently Clint eased the lever of his Winchester down and back up. The twin clicks were muffled. Clint lifted the cocked weapon to his shoulder and straightened to his feet. He set the Winchester's sights on the gambler.

"Time to fold, Rancon," he said loud enough to carry.

For a bare second Rancon went rigid. Then he pivoted in a tight crouch, firing wildly as he turned. Clint shot him through the chest. The butt of the Winchester kicked against Clint's shoulder. Rancon went over sideward. In a small landslide of dirt and gravel, his body rolled and slid lifelessly down the hill and dropped from sight into the gully where Handley had hidden himself.

Clint stepped back into concealment. No shots sounded. No bullets snapped by his head. Apparently his gunplay with Rancon hadn't revealed his presence to the remaining outlaw, wherever he was.

Staying to cover, he catfooted down the hill to the natural fortress that had sheltered him and Brandon. There was no sign of the gun boss except a litter of cartridge cases. But his horse was still nearby. Brandon must have gone in search of the third member of the outlaw trio.

Clint retrieved his hat and padded back up into cover on the lower slope of the hill. He began to work his way warily around its base. The last echoes of gunfire had long since died, but the air still felt tense and expectant.

A shadow flashed over his face, and he looked up to see a huge vulture skimming past low overhead. He wondered how long it would be before the scavenger and its brethren settled down on the bodies he'd left behind him.

A flurry of shots came from the far side of the hill. Clint recognized the rapid-fire action of Brandon's pistol merged with the slower reports of a Colt. He went more swiftly, although he still used the scattered rocks and brush for concealment.

The sound of voices reached him. In another few seconds he drew up short at a grim sight. Brandon had his pistol in his fist. Buck was down on his knees before him, his right shoulder bloody. His lean face was twisted in pain and fear. Whatever kind of showdown the two men had had, it was clear that Brandon had come out on top.

"I figured you'd be back here trying to make off with the gold like the no-good horse thief you are," Brandon boasted. "So I just came around to head you off. Beats me why I ever hired you, Buck."

Looking beyond them, Clint could see three weary horses and a metal strongbox beside them. Buck must have been covering his partners' backsides. He had tried to cut and run when he figured that their luck had played out.

"Honest, Mr. Brandon," he babbled now, clutching his wounded shoulder, "Rancon and Handley forced me to help them! I didn't want nothing to do with crossing you, Mr. Brandon!"

"That's about the sorriest lie I ever heard," Brandon told him. His tone was regretful. "I guess I didn't make myself clear the other night. You're fired."

His pistol stabbed an ear-splitting flame. Buck toppled over and lay still.

A coldness gripped Clint's soul. There had been no chance for him to take a hand. He hadn't expected Brandon to act quite so fast or quite so ruthlessly.

Brandon swung his head around. His face held the violence of some pagan savage. Something of Clint's feelings must have been written on his face.

"That kind of justice bother you, Bradlock?" Brandon demanded.

Clint forced a shrug. "Just one more body to bury."

"Bury?" Brandon echoed. "We're taking all three of these bushwhackers back draped across their saddles. I'll show White City it doesn't pay to tangle with Carter Brandon!"

In the firelight Brandon's face was all sharp-edged flint. He paused in cleaning his pistol with an oily rag and looked across at Clint. "You lived up to your rep out there today," he jibed. "What about it? You think you're fast enough to take a man armed with a semi-automatic pistol like this?''

Clint was cleaning his own rifle. ''Depends on the man, I guess.'' He continued reaming out the barrel of his Winchester.

Brandon held the gun so that the flames glinted off the dark metal. Like his face, the weapon looked hard and deadly. ''You ever seen one of these before?''

Clint glanced at the pistol. ''I recollect it's a Bergmann. Takes a nine-shot magazine.''

Brief, ugly displeasure twisted Brandon's thin mouth. Then he grinned grudgingly. ''I should have guessed Clint Bradlock would know the tools of his trade.'' He hefted the Bergmann thoughtfully. ''This will shoot faster and reload faster than any revolver ever made. It'd give even a greenhorn a chance against a *pistolero,* if he knew how to use it. You mark my words. One day this type of pistol will make Mr. Colt's revolver obsolete.''

Clint kept his own counsel. From hooded eyes he gazed across the flames at the other man. In a sense, his job was done. He had the gold, and he knew who was behind the outlaw campaign against Howard Herns. Of course, he didn't know why Brandon was preying on Herns. But given time, Brandon would talk if he was in the hands of the authorities. All that remained was for him to take Brandon into custody and return him and the gold to Guthrie. But taking him into custody wouldn't be any Sunday social, and the Bergmann might play a part in the deal.

What would happen in White City if Brandon was no longer in charge? Clint wondered. More particularly, what would happen to Elaine if her guardian failed to return? Clint recalled the way Sledger had eyed her. He thought next of the human predators inhabiting White City. The idea of Elaine alone there even now was almost intolerable.

Bleakly he put aside the idea of trying to overpower Brandon. Whatever his obligation to the Partners, he knew he couldn't ride off and leave Elaine defenseless in White City.

He and Brandon had made their camp in a sheltered niche on the side of the hill. Their horses and the horses of the outlaws were hobbled nearby. The bodies had been laid out to be taken back tomorrow.

Clint's stomach still wallowed at the memory of the cold-blooded murder he had witnessed. With no appetite, he had chewed on a strip of jerky while Brandon wolfed down hard biscuits and salted ham. Clint tried not to let his eyes stray to the black strongbox squatting at the edge of the firelight. So far the gold had cost the lives of five men. He wondered if it would end up costing his own as well.

He noted that Brandon had fallen to staring moodily at the strongbox. His earlier sneering attitude appeared to have soured. He pulled out his hip flask and drank from it. "Dead bodies out in the night, no roof over our heads, and stale food," he said morosely. "This ain't the life for a gentleman."

"Vanity of vanities. All is vanity," Clint murmured dryly.

Brandon's head jerked up sharply. His eyes glittered dangerously. "You think that's funny?"

"Just quoting the Good Book," Clint drawled.

Brandon scowled into the night. "White City ain't the end of the line for me, Bradlock. You can put your money on it."

"You got plans, do you?"

"*Big* plans," Brandon confirmed with feeling. "This territory is opening up. Statehood's not too many years away, and when it comes, there won't be any place for towns like White City or for men like us."

Men like us. The words echoed somberly in Clint's mind. He recalled his earlier feelings of kinship with this man. Was that what he had become over the hard, violent years—a man like Carter Brandon?

"Someone with the right kind of resources and guts and brains can make a new start and leave his past behind him," Brandon resumed.

"Are you planning to go respectable?" Clint asked with a ring of irony.

"Sure, you think it's funny, but that's because you don't have the vision that I do. Also, that's the reason you work for me and not the other way around. I've planned things for a good long time now. This gold's just part of it. I've been getting together the kind of resources I need to start over. That's why I never wanted to own any of the two-bit dives in White City. I don't care to have those kind of ties when it's time for me to move on. I'll be able to go into any type of business I want, maybe into politics. Oklahoma will have senators and representatives just like the other states. I might set my sights on an office like that. And from there, who knows what I could do?''

Stranger things had happened, Clint reckoned. With wealth to buy a facade of respectability, many an unscrupulous man with a shady past had achieved great heights of success and power in business and politics. Brandon had the charm and ruthless strength to go a long way, particularly in a raw and brawling new state like Oklahoma would soon become.

The idea didn't set well. Whatever Oklahoma's future was to be, Clint figured, it shouldn't be placed in the unscrupulous hands of men like Brandon.

But there were answers here too, he sensed, answers needed if he was to bring Brandon down. ''You sound like a wealthy man,'' he prodded with a careful edge of skepticism.

''You think that gold alone doesn't make me wealthy?'' Brandon asserted. ''And that's only part of it. I've been taking from people who can afford to lose some of their holdings in these parts. More than that, they deserve to lose them.'' His lips curled like those of a hungry wolf. ''Best part is, I'm settling an old score, to boot.''

''What kind of score?''

Brandon pulled at his flask again. He stared into the fire for a long moment. ''There was a time when I wasn't too different from you—living by my gun, hiring myself out, maybe going after bounty money if it was good enough, and always watching my back. I had a pretty good reputation, and it got the attention of some gentlemen from back East. They were looking for a man who could handle a six-shooter and keep his mouth shut. Seems they'd acquired a lot of property and assets out here in the Territory, with an eye to the future when statehood comes through. They needed an hombre to look out after their interests. It had to be someone who knew the Territory and could fit into it. Someone who could take matters into his own hands, if need be, to protect their interests. They called themselves the Partners.''

With an effort, Clint forced his face to remain impassive. Brandon was so caught up in his tale that he didn't seem to notice any effect his words had had on his listener. ''Like some kind of range detective?'' Clint asked hollowly.

Brandon nodded. ''Something like that, only I wasn't to let on that I worked for them. They figured I'd be better able to keep an eye on things and pick up information if nobody suspected me of being on their payroll. To anybody looking on, I was just another shiftless gun hand. Not bad work all in all. And they paid me a right pretty penny for doing it.''

So Brandon had been his predecessor, Clint mused, living a life that was half a lie and acting a role that could be fatal if he missed his cues.

''Working for the Partners gave me a taste for the good things,'' Brandon went on. ''I got to see what it's like to have money and power enough to buy and sell men like you and me. That's what makes a gentleman, Bradlock—having enough money and power so that no one can call your hand.''

"How'd you end up at White City?" Clint asked casually.

"I got crossways with one of the Partners," Brandon snarled. "I recovered some of his cattle from a pack of no-account rustlers, and he had the gall to say I'd handled it wrong."

"How's that?"

"There were five rustlers. I got the drop on them and had them dead to rights. But there wasn't any way I could take all of them in and get the cattle back as well. I sure wasn't going to leave five owlhoots running around loose to turn around and cause me more grief."

"So you killed them," Clint said flatly.

"Any self-respecting judge and jury would have hanged them anyway! They were nothing but back-shooting trash, all of them!"

"I guess your bosses didn't see it that way."

"What did they know?" Brandon demanded vehemently. "Had any of them ever been under the gun? Or tracked a killer on a cold trail?"

"Reckon not."

"And the worst of the bunch is that sorry beggar, Herns."

"Who?" Clint asked with as much indifference as he could muster.

"Howard Herns, one of the Partners. He saw to it that I was fired. You ever heard of him?"

"Can't say that I have."

"He's the boss dog in the pack. When he found out what had happened, he told the others that they didn't have any business hiring a vigilante and a murderer. Shoot! It was his blamed stock I was recovering!"

"So they cut you loose."

"Yeah," Brandon growled. "After me risking my life to protect their sorry livestock and ranches, they fired me like I was some two-bit cowpuncher!"

"You're doing all right in White City," Clint commented. "Looks to me like things worked out."

"Not well enough to suit me, they didn't!" Brandon stormed. "Some of the owners of White City had heard of me. They offered me the job of maintaining order there so that the customers didn't keep getting killed. They told me I could pretty much have a free hand. So I made some rules and backed them up with my gun. I killed three men my first three days there. Then I hired some fellows who knew one end of a gun from the other, and told them to enforce my rules. Didn't take long after that for things to settle down. I set up the free prizefights and cockfights, and provided places for the drunks to sleep off their binges. It worked like a charm."

"What made you go after Herns?"

"I never figured to ride herd on that trouble town forever. I had men on the payroll who answered only to me. I thought of Herns sitting back East, all fat and sassy, with his lands and cattle and gold out here just waiting to be plucked. I knew all about what he owned. Heck, I used to guard it all! And since it was Herns that caused me to end up in White City, I decided he could be the one to give me a way out and the means to start over.'' Brandon chuckled harshly. ''I been worrying at him like a lobo wolf after a fat steer. I'd give a lot to see his face and let him know it was me putting the spurs to him.''

Apparently Brandon wasn't aware that Herns was in the Territory. ''How long you going to keep hounding him?'' Clint asked.

Brandon brooded darkly for a moment. ''I've almost got what I need out of his sorry hide,'' he admitted finally. ''But I'd like to get in at least one more good lick at him before I let him go, one that he won't ever forget!''

''Have you kicked his dog yet? Sounds like there ain't much left for you to do to him.''

''I'll find something,'' Brandon vowed. ''I got people watching and listening to keep me informed on all his business.''

''They must have let you down the other day. I counted you two men short when you came back.''

Brandon frowned. ''There was something right odd about that deal. We were going after a payroll being shipped on a freight line Herns owns, but they had it guarded coming and going. Wasn't no way to get ahold of it.''

Clint sensed the capable hand of Thom Chancery,

at work safeguarding the interests of Howard Herns. "Maybe you're pushing your luck," he said carefully. "Could be a good idea to back off. Appears to me you've done him a heap of harm already."

Brandon shook his head stubbornly. "It's not enough," he declared flatly. "Not enough harm done to him, and not enough money for my plans."

"You could leave White City tomorrow," Clint persisted. "You could go anywhere you want to start over."

"Not the way I plan to do it. I'll set things up right. One day I'll be hiring and firing men like us."

"You already are," Clint pointed out.

"It's not the same!"

Clint studied Brandon's hard face, and in the wavering light of the fire, it seemed for an instant as if he were gazing at some distorted reflection of himself—a little older, a little more bitter and cynical, and with all the compassion leached out of him. The night had turned cold. Was this what awaited him a few years and a few more gunfights down the trail?

Brandon turned thoughtful. "Respectability's a big part of it," he mused aloud. "A gentleman, a man of means, needs a nice home and a proper wife that'll do him credit. I've got the right woman picked out too."

"You talking about Rhonda?"

Brandon sneered. "Rhonda's like a blanket. When it gets worn out, you throw it away. No, I'm talking about a real lady with some culture and refinement to her."

A slow, ugly horror writhed up in Clint. "Who might that be?" He tried to keep his voice level.

Brandon grinned, his teeth flashing like fangs in the firelight. "Who do you think? You know her. Elaine, of course. Why do you suppose I'm keeping her in that big house with a bodyguard at the door? When she's of age in a couple of months, I'll marry her, all proper and legal. She'd make a good wife for a man of means. I had the idea the minute I saw her after her pa died."

"She's your niece, man!" Clint said hoarsely.

"Not by blood. Or even by law. She's my foster brother's girl—no real relation to me."

"She might have something to say about that." Clint remembered Elaine telling him of Brandon's changing attitude toward her.

"No. I'll talk to her about it beforehand," Brandon said confidently. "Even if she doesn't like the idea at first, she'll come around. Besides, what choice does she have? She doesn't have anybody else to look after her but me."

And what were his own choices? Clint asked himself. Whatever obligations he had to Herns and the Partners, he knew that he had a higher responsibility now. Somehow, whatever the cost, he had to get Elaine away from White City and out of the clutches of Carter Brandon before all her choices were made for her.

Chapter Nine

"We've identified the two outlaws killed in the attempted robbery of the freight line, Mr. Herns," Thom Chancery reported. "Unfortunately, that doesn't tell us a great deal. As with the men who stole the gold shipment, these were nothing but gunmen with the reputation of being available to the highest bidder."

"That's unfortunate." The fleshy face of the Eastern millionaire was furrowed and thoughtful. "Still, I'm glad we implemented your idea of increasing the guards on all such shipments." He leaned back in the leather chair behind the heavy oak desk. "That was good planning. It saved us from being the victims of another robbery."

"Thank you, sir." Beneath his feet and through the frame of the upholstered chair in which he sat, Chancery could feel the faint vibration of movement. He was accustomed to it, as he was accustomed to the constant muffled roar of the steam locomotive thundering down the tracks. The office space here in the opulent private railroad car of Howard Herns wasn't large, but it was lavishly furnished, as were all the millionaire's traveling headquarters for his tour of his Western holdings.

Chancery estimated that the Pullman car had cost Herns close to one hundred thousand dollars. In addition to the office space, it had sleeping arrangements for three, servant's quarters, storage, a parlor, a bathroom complete with bathtub, and a small smoking room. Named after George Pullman, their designer, such cars were earmarks of the wealth and success of their owners.

"Has there been any word from Bradlock?" Herns asked now.

"No, sir, but that's hardly surprising. He hasn't been gone much over a week. With White City being what it is, he may not be able to get any kind of message to us, even if he wanted to risk it. I wouldn't worry. He's reliable and can take care of himself." But, he admitted to himself, sending Bradlock to White City smacked of setting a single wolfhound against a whole pack of wolves.

Herns grunted and reached for the cord to draw the heavy drapes over the window. Through the glass, Chancery had a view of the flat plains country across which they traveled. They were still a good two hours out of Oklahoma City, he estimated. The train ride from Guthrie would take most of the afternoon. They wouldn't be arriving until late in the day.

"Have you scheduled the dinner meeting with the bankers?" Herns inquired.

Chancery nodded. "It's all set." He knew that Herns was hoping to buy the Oklahoma City bank. The deal had temporarily fallen through after the theft of the gold shipment intended for that purpose.

"You'll be present, of course." Herns was polite enough to make a comment out of the command.

"Yes, sir."

Dinner meetings with millionaires and bank owners, Chancery reflected silently. He had come a long way for an ex-New York City police officer. As the official representative for the Partners, and sometime business manager of their holdings in the Territory, he daily wielded a great deal of influence and power under the authority of his employers. But though he appreciated some of the trappings of their great wealth, he had never seriously aspired to join their ranks. Men like Herns, he had long since decided, were owned by their stock and business enterprises and land and other investments rather than the other way around. Instead of controlling their assets, they were, in a sense, controlled by them. To Herns and the other Partners, losing their lives might almost be preferable to losing their wealth. The fight to preserve and increase their holdings gave them their purpose for existence.

That type of life was not for Chancery. He would be satisfied with his handsome salary and the ability, if need be, to walk away from the wealth he assisted his employers in managing. Even should the Partners grow dissatisfied with his services, he was confident of his ability to find employment in any one of a dozen different trades.

His part-time work as a bodyguard for one of the Partners had first brought him to the attention of the cartel of elite businessmen. At the time, he had still been employed as a police officer. If nothing else, he was sure he could go back to working as a bodyguard or obtain employment at one of the large detective agencies whose services he sometimes used on behalf of the Partners. Perhaps he might even start his own agency.

So maybe he hadn't come very far after all, he mused. Without reaching to touch it, he was aware of the shortened barrel, single-action Colt .38 revolver in the shoulder holster beneath his tailored suit coat. He was rarely without the weapon, and still practiced regularly with it although he hadn't been called on to use it in years.

"Well, I suppose things are in order." Herns closed the ledger on the desk before him and rose to his feet. "Care for a drink?"

"Just a small one, sir."

Chancery followed Herns into the small smoking room, where there was a fully stocked bar. Geoffrey, Herns's gray-haired butler, appeared before them. Herns issued crisp orders for their drinks.

"Right away, sir." Geoffrey's British origins were and always would be evident in his clipped accent. He moved smoothly behind the bar and produced a bottle and glasses. He was a wiry man with a small mustache, and Chancery knew he had served in the British military before entering the service of his present employer.

Herns settled into a comfortable chair upholstered in soft leather. Like much of the furniture in the car, it was bolted to the floor. He gestured for Chancery to join him. As Chancery sat down, his eyes turned to the two expensive big-bore hunting rifles mounted on the wall. Herns appreciated quality even in his firearms.

Geoffrey served their drinks and retired discreetly to the bar. Herns sipped from his glass, then gazed reflectively at the countryside outside the window.

"Can Bradlock be trusted not to take matters into his own hands?" he asked abruptly.

"I'd say so," Chancery told him. "When he has apprehended lawbreakers in the past, he's always been faithful in turning them over to the authorities, if possible."

Herns nodded with apparent satisfaction. "That's good. I'd hate to have another episode such as that one a few years back, where our man killed those rustlers in cold blood."

"I don't think we need to worry on that count." Chancery paused diplomatically before changing the subject. "Do you have any plans for after we leave Oklahoma City? I may need to make arrangements."

"We'll be heading up to Liberal," Herns answered. "I'd like to make personal contact with some of the cattle buyers there."

"I'll see to accommodations in Liberal when we

reach Oklahoma City. And I'll also advise the crew of our plans.''

''Tomorrow afternoon will probably be the earliest we would leave. You can have the crew standing by then.''

''I'll take care of it.''

Though the Pullman coach belonged to Herns, the engine that pulled it was the property of the Santa Fe Railroad. Along with the two crewmen, it was on loan to Herns at the direction of one of his fellow Partners who was on the board of the railroad.

Chancery pictured a map of the Territory in his mind's eye. En route to Liberal they would pass not far from White City. He tasted his drink and wondered what progress, if any, Clint Bradlock had made on his assignment there.

From the open window of her upstairs sitting room, Elaine could see Clint and Carter when they rode back into White City. She had been watching most of the day, hoping and praying for their swift and safe return. Now, as she saw the three limp forms slung over the saddles of the horses they led, she felt a shudder of horror.

She put it aside, and let her eyes rest on Clint Bradlock as he walked his horse past. She fancied that he glanced quickly toward the house. A foolish tingle touched her spine, although she was sure he could not see her through the lace curtains.

He looked worn and haggard, she thought, as if the

journey had taken a great toll on him. She felt a sudden urge to comfort him despite the worries that preyed upon her.

Carter, by contrast, was making his black gelding almost prance beneath him, as if he were riding in a parade. He made her think of a conquering general of some pagan army returning from the field of battle. His head was high. His body had an arrogant set to it.

When would Clint be coming to the house? Soon, she prayed.

A crowd of men was gathering from the gaming halls. They viewed the bodies excitedly. Elaine saw Sledger stride out from the house to join them. She knew an irrational sense of relief. Although he had made no more improper overtures toward her, the fighter had rarely stirred from the front porch since his invasion of her parlor. His presence had lurked like an evil spirit over the house.

She saw Clint dismount inconspicuously and ease clear of the gathering. He led his horses away toward the stable. Behind him, Carter, still mounted, seemed to be playing to the crowd and enjoying their adulation. He angled his horse down the street toward the center of town. He was still leading the other horses with their grisly burdens. The crowd surged along with him. She could hear the ugly rumble of their drunken voices. Sledger detached himself and came striding easily back toward the house.

Elaine bit her lip in vexation. She had hoped that Carter would come here immediately. Obviously, such was not to be the case. She would just have to wait. But, at least for the time being, she was safe. Sledger would never dare try anything while Carter was in town.

She had known from the first that she had to tell Carter of what had happened. To remain silent out of fear would be the first step in succumbing to Sledger's vile extortion of her body and soul. She would not allow that to happen. The short-term risk of Sledger's wrath was far outweighed by the potential damage, physical and mental, he might do to her over the long run.

She sighed as she watched the crowd follow a triumphant Carter out of sight down the street. She would just have to continue to wait for him, she told herself again. To leave the house and go in search of him was out of the question, even if Sledger would permit it.

Time limped past for her. She tried to fill it with her books. Somehow, she couldn't bring herself to play the piano. The light tunes, she was certain, were beyond her abilities today, and the somber ones would only add to her gloom.

She read listlessly through *The Vicar of Wakefield*, a novel by Oliver Goldsmith. She had to force her mind to concentrate. Anxiety vied with musing over Clint Bradlock's whereabouts and activities.

Two men arrived, lugging a heavy strongbox. From her window she watched them and heard them tell Sledger that Carter had sent the box over. Grudgingly, Sledger took it from them and hefted it to his shoulder in a frightening display of strength. She heard him store it downstairs.

She stirred again at the sound of a rapidly ridden horse pulling to a halt in front of the house. Curious, she rose and moved to the window. Dusk was falling, but she could make out a shabby man on a winded horse just outside the picket fence.

"Is Mr. Brandon in there, Sledger?" he shouted.

"Naw. I reckon he's down at the Elephant," Sledger grumbled. "Why you asking?"

"I got important news! He'll be wanting to hear it pronto!"

Sledger had grunted a response she couldn't hear, and the horseman turned his horse and kicked it into a tired trot.

Elaine drew back from the window. More of Carter's obscure business dealings, she reflected with distaste. Sentimental novels held no more interest for her. Vieja would be preparing dinner, she thought with sudden inspiration. Maybe she could be of assistance in that task.

It wasn't until after dinner that Carter appeared at the house. She heard him enter, and hurried into the parlor to greet him. He loomed big and authoritative in the room. If anything, the air of aggressive triumph she had noted earlier set on him even more firmly now. He had changed out of his range clothes into a gentleman's suit, and he looked quite dashing in it. She wondered vaguely what occasion prompted his more formal attire. She knew that he virtually lived at the

Elephant Saloon, and she suspected he had a woman there although she didn't like to dwell on the matter.

"I'm so glad to see you!" she exclaimed breathlessly.

"And I'm glad to see you, honey." His smile flashed as he took her hands and swept her smoothly to the love seat. "You look enchanting tonight. Sit down. We need to talk."

She allowed herself to be seated. He settled beside her, closer than she cared for him to be. He continued to hold one of her hands firmly in his. The foul smell of whiskey was on his breath.

"I have to tell you—" she started.

"Hush," he ordered gently. "Whatever it is, it can wait." He seemed oblivious to the urgency in her tone. "I've been needing to talk to you, and tonight's a good time to do it. I've just gotten news that should allow me to make arrangements for us to leave White City."

"Oh, that's wonderful—" she began, but he cut her off by pressing a finger to her lips. She didn't like the intimacy of the gesture. She tried to draw back, but his grip held her easily.

"Listen to me," he ordered, and went on before she could respond. "I've been watching you. You've grown into a lovely woman, and it's not right for you to be shut up in this big house in a place like White City." He leaned forward intently. She wanted to avoid his eyes but couldn't. His voice was smooth and persuasive. "I've never really thought of you as a relative of mine, Elaine. We aren't really related, you know.

When we were both younger, I always thought of you
as a friend of mine. But since you've come back from
school, I've realized that you're no longer a child.
You're a woman, and you need a man to look after
you and protect you.''

''Uncle Carter—'' she began desperately.

''No,'' he said quietly. ''It's not 'Uncle' anymore.
It's just 'Carter.' I've told you that. We're both
adults.''

Black horror welled up in her soul as he continued
to speak. She felt trapped and paralyzed as his smooth,
awful words pushed relentlessly into her benumbed
mind.

''We'll get married proper at a church,'' he finished.
''I know you'll want that. I'll treat you like a queen,
Elaine. There'll be only the best for Mrs. Carter Bran-
don. No more towns like White City. We'll go in style.
I promise you that!''

At last he released her hand and rose. She wilted
back into the love seat. He towered over her like some
dark, evil god.

''There's no rush,'' he assured her. ''We'll have to
wait until after your birthday, and I realize you need
a little time to get used to the idea.''

He fell silent, and for one horrible moment she
thought he would bend over and try to kiss her. But
he seemed to have second thoughts. He stepped back,
gave her one last flashing smile, and strode from the
room. She heard the front door close behind him.

She imagined she could feel the defiling touch of

his finger on her lips. She felt like a squirrel in a cage as her mind raced in frantic and useless circles. She had been betrayed and violated. In the back of her mind, she realized that she had never even mentioned Sledger and his threats. It didn't matter. In his own way, Carter Brandon offered an even greater and more horrifying menace. She was trapped between two evils.

She had only one hope, and that was Clint Bradlock. Somehow, she must get word to him.

Clint stepped out of the Elephant and breathed deeply of the night air. His head ached from the foul haze of cigarette smoke, alcohol fumes, sweat, and the dust that hung like a cloud inside the saloon. The brassy piano music was almost smothered by the crude shouts and laughter of the bar's drunken patrons and the saloon girls preying on them.

Where was Brandon? he wondered. The gun boss had disappeared from the festivities in the saloon after a sorry-looking stranger had brought him some news.

Clint glanced up the street toward the big house. Almost of their own will, his feet headed him toward it. As a figure flitted out of the darkness of an alley, Clint turned sharply with a hand going for his gun. His nerves were still strung taut in the aftermath of the deadly stalk on the rocky hill. Then he recognized the gaunt silhouette of Vieja, the old Indian woman. He forced his fingers to relax from the butt of his Colt. Vieja motioned him forward urgently. Warily he stepped into the alley. He remembered her big bowie knife.

"You come," she commanded, and jerked her head in the direction he had been traveling. "Miss Elaine need you. Now!"

She started to turn away with the last emphatic word, but Clint caught her by a bony shoulder. "Wait! What's wrong?"

She shrugged free of his hand with surprising strength. "You come!" She shuffled off.

He followed her stooped, ghostly figure as she led him through shadowy byways and paths. At last they drew close to the rear of the house. For a moment she paused, like a wild animal on the alert for enemies. Then she motioned him to follow her. In his mind's eye he pictured Sledger sitting on the front porch, shotgun at hand. He was risking a lot to come here in such fashion, but he could not resist the mysterious summons.

At the foot of the back steps, she stopped and waved him on toward the door. He understood she was positioning herself here outside as a guard.

He mounted the steps two at a time. The screened outer door swung open and he saw Elaine in the dimness inside. He realized she had been waiting for him. Impulsively, she caught his hand and drew him into the hallway. Suddenly, then, she was hugging him with a frantic strength. His arms went around her, easy and natural.

"Thank God you're here," she gasped against his

chest. "I sent Vieja to find you, but I didn't know if she could."

Clint was conscious of the screened door at his back. Gently he shifted her out of the hallway and into the gloom of the kitchen. Then he said softly, still holding her, "What's wrong?"

She told him everything about Sledger and Brandon in broken, stumbling phrases, and he felt his muscles bunch and tighten. "I don't know what to do!" she finished. She drew back to gaze up at him. In the dim light he could see the tears glinting on her cheeks.

He caught her shoulders with firm, gentle hands. "Listen to me," he said. "I'll get you out of here. I won't let Sledger or Brandon, either one, hurt you." He paused. He knew he was about to break one of his own rules for survival, but he also knew that he had to do it. He didn't want there to be lies and deception between them any longer. "I don't really work for Brandon. I'm here on a job for some important men from back East. It all has to do with Brandon." Clint drew a deep breath. "He's involved in some illegal activities. Part of my job is to stop him and turn him over to the authorities, if possible."

She shut her eyes and sagged briefly in his grip. "I was sure you weren't like the rest of them," she said when she lifted her gaze to him. "There was something about you that was clean and decent under all the weapons and the hard talk. And I've known that Carter had to be involved in something dishonest or illegal. I just never wanted to admit it to myself."

Clint enclosed her in his arms. She came willingly. "I'm almost finished here," he told her. "As soon as I am, we'll leave. I'll take you out of White City and see to it that Brandon and Sledger never touch you."

She trembled in his arms. "I knew you would," she murmured.

He eased her back so that he could look down at her pale, upturned face. She was a breathtaking image in the dimness. "We'll have to be careful," he advised quietly. "The safest time to leave will be when Brandon is gone. Otherwise, he'll have half the town after us."

"What about Sledger?"

"I'll handle Sledger," Clint said tightly. And he vowed to himself that, one way or another, he'd deal with Brandon as well.

She leaned her head against his chest. "I'm glad you're here. I was so scared. I didn't know what to do. I didn't have anywhere to turn."

Clint stroked her black hair. It was as smooth as the night under his palm. He was conscious of her closeness against him. "You have me," he said softly. "You'll always have me." He hadn't planned the words, but now that he'd said them, they seemed good and right, and he didn't want to take them back.

She lifted her face and stared up at him with searching, questioning eyes. She seemed to find the answers she needed. Her arms tightened about him.

Again he didn't plan it. He bent his head and lowered

his mouth to her upturned lips. They were soft and warm and yielding.

At last he disentangled himself. "I have to get out of here," he said, "but be ready to leave. I'll try to get word to warn you early, but the next time Brandon leaves, I'll come for you. Meanwhile, I'll be close by."

"I know you will," she whispered. "I know."

Chapter Ten

"Where the deuce have you been?" Brandon demanded from his customary table in the Elephant.

Clint shrugged. "Checking on things," he said. Elaine's parting kiss was still warm on his lips.

Brandon didn't press him for details. "Something's come up. I've been making plans."

Clint recalled the messenger who had brought Brandon news earlier in the evening. He pulled out a chair. "Tell me about it," he said as he seated himself.

Brandon's grin was predatory. "Remember I told you I was waiting for the right chance to pull one final job against Herns?"

"Yeah. So?"

"So the right chance is here," Brandon answered with relish. "I just got word that Herns himself is in the Territory and looking over his holdings."

Tension tightened Clint's muscles. He waited for Brandon to continue.

"Not only is he here," Brandon obliged him, "but

he's traveling on his private train, and right now he's en route from Oklahoma City to Liberal, Kansas.''

Clint began to get an ugly inkling, and he didn't like it. ''You planning something?''

''You bet I am!'' Brandon leaned forward intently and propped his forearms on the table. A half-filled bottle of whiskey was at his elbow. No glass was in sight. ''The rail line runs east of here. You know what that means? Herns himself, the boss dog of the Partners, is going to be passing within a few score miles of this very spot.'' Brandon showed his teeth in a grinning snarl. ''I plan to be there to meet the train!''

''In Liberal?'' Clint said, although he already had a better than sneaking suspicion of what Brandon planned to do.

''No! Out on the range!'' Brandon snapped. ''Me and a bunch of the boys are going to stop that train and take Mr. Boss Dog Herns off it, just as pretty as you please!''

''And kill him?'' Clint probed.

''Not first thing,'' Brandon answered, low and mean. ''Leastways, not until he's made some arrangements back East. They'll be for me to be paid five hundred thousand dollars to turn him loose!''

''What if he pays?''

''Either way, he ends up dead. 'Course, he won't know that until after the money is in my hands.''

''Do you think you can get away with kidnapping a man like that, holding him for ransom, and then killing him, to boot?''

"What's going to stop me? Once we have him, I'll bring him straight to White City. There's no law here but what I make. The U.S. marshals don't have any authority."

He was right, Clint thought grimly. Regardless of whether any ransom was paid, whatever rescue attempt might be organized would be too late for Herns. "Just where is the rail line?" He tried to keep the strain from his voice.

"It runs pretty much north and south. You head out of here due east and eventually you'll run into it."

Clint remembered the line from his knowledge of the Territory. Mentally he berated Chancery and Herns for being fools enough to pass that close to White City. But even he had never foreseen a daring strike such as Brandon now proposed. He knew it would do no good to try to dissuade him. "When are you riding out?"

"Soon as I get enough of the boys together. Ratter is taking care of that now. I'll leave a few men here. I want you to stay and keep an eye on things for me."

Clint nodded easily. "Sure."

"What are you doing, honey?" Rhonda asked as she sidled up to the table by Brandon's chair.

Brandon cut her a look that was almost contemptuous. "I'm busy," he dismissed her curtly.

Rhonda's eyes flashed. She turned to flounce away. Brandon ignored her and drank deeply from the whiskey bottle. Then he set it down hard and rose to his feet. "I'm going to see what's keeping Ratter."

Clint watched him stride from the saloon. Things

were starting to move like a stampede, and he had the feeling that he was right in its path.

He had to stop Brandon, but he also had to get Elaine out of White City. She needed to be warned that events were breaking faster than he'd expected, but he couldn't risk going to see her again at this point. He rose quickly, his mind churning.

Sledger was a bulky figure in the gloom of the porch when Clint reached the house. Light from the open windows glinted off the barrels of his shotgun.

"You want something, Bradlock?" His hoarse voice was surly.

"Brandon's fixing to ride out." As Clint raised his voice louder than was necessary, he hoped that Elaine and Vieja were within earshot inside the house. "He's taking a bunch of the boys with him. He's got some kind of major job planned. Thought you'd like to know."

"I already heard. You got any other business here?"

"I reckon not."

Sledger grunted. Clint made himself turn and amble away. He didn't fancy offering his vulnerable back to Sledger's shotgun, but by acting wary he might put Sledger on his guard.

He drew a sigh of relief as he moved out of range. Had Elaine or Vieja been close enough to the window to hear him? Would they understand the significance of his words? One way or another, his work here was going to be finished tonight.

Up ahead, about a dozen men and their horses were

gathering in front of the Elephant. The sounds of their excited voices reached him. As he drew closer, he saw Brandon swing up astride a horse.

"Get your tails in the saddle!" the gun boss bellowed.

As the men mounted, Brandon saw Clint, and he pulled up so hard on his reins that his horse reared. "Look after things!" he ordered.

Clint replied with a wordless salute, forefinger to the brim of his Stetson.

"Come on, men, move out!"

Clint stepped to the side of the street as Brandon led his crew past at a gallop. Their rowdy shouts and cries echoed from the flimsy facades of the buildings. Clint tasted the gritty dust of their passage.

He waited until their hoofbeats faded. A sense of urgency was beginning to gnaw at him, but he couldn't afford to make mistakes now.

He reentered the saloon and scanned its occupants until he spotted the flame of Rhonda's hair at the far end of the bar. A bottle and glass were in front of her. She was alone. No cowpokes were seeking her favors. Word was out that it was a fool's move to mess with Brandon's woman.

Clint threaded his way through the crowd in her direction. She ignored him as he put his back to the bar beside her. His eyes continued to roam the hazy room. He spotted the furtive figure of Ratter lurking in a corner.

"Drinking alone?" He barely moved his lips as he spoke to her.

"What's it to you?" Her voice was slurred.

Clint could sense Ratter's eyes on them, and he jerked his head toward the rear of the saloon. "Five minutes. Brandon's office," he said.

She gave him a quick, surprised look and then turned away. "What are you playing at?"

"You want Brandon all to yourself or don't you?" Before she could answer, he pushed off from the bar and headed toward the door to the rear of the building. He could feel her eyes on his back, and he knew that she could be almost as dangerous as the barrels of Sledger's shotgun.

The door to Brandon's makeshift office had not been repaired. Clint knew that Brandon had arranged for the gold to be placed in the house under Sledger's guard. He lit a lantern and left the door to the office only slightly ajar. He fancied the scent of death still hung in the room.

He was counting on Rhonda's curiosity and jealousy to bring her, and he wasn't disappointed. In a few minutes she pushed the door open and was standing in the doorway.

"I'm here," she said. "But don't get any wrong ideas. Carter would kill any man who touched me."

"Relax. Your virtue is safe with me," Clint drawled. He motioned her into the room.

She came forward and pushed the door shut behind

her without further urging. She eyed Clint suspiciously. "So, what do you want?"

"Do you know who I am?"

"You're Carter's *segundo*," she sneered. "Big man."

"This has to do with his ward, Elaine Allison."

The name set her off like a spark touching black powder. "Ward, my foot!" she snarled contemptuously. "That finishing-school tart! Little Miss Pure and Innocent! I know darned well what Carter's planning with her. One of these days he'll up and take her out of here and marry her so he can live respectable, and I won't have nothing to show for my devotion but his bootprints!" Her face had turned ugly. "If it wasn't for her, if it wasn't for this blamed stinking town, I'd be the one he was planning to marry! But instead, she's got him and doesn't even know it!"

"She knows," Clint said softly.

Rhonda's tirade broke off abruptly.

"I'm fixing to leave town with her. Now. Tonight. She doesn't want any part of marrying her guardian."

Rhonda stared at him skeptically. "You're serious?"

"I'm real serious."

"Carter'll be after you like a hawk on a rat!"

Clint shrugged. "He'll have to catch us first. Besides, what do you care? At least it's a chance to be rid of her."

She dropped her eyes broodingly. For a moment he saw a ghost of a lovely and innocent young woman. "I hate this town," she said, so softly that he barely caught her words. "This one and all the others like it, with their honky-tonks and whiskey and fast-living men. They can steal a girl's soul." Her voice hardened. "And this town is the worst. It's the end of the line. If Carter leaves me here, I'll never escape. I know I won't."

"I need your help."

She studied him. "What do you mean?"

"I'll have to deal with Sledger. I hope I can do it quietly. But whatever happens, I can't afford to have any of Brandon's enforcers get involved."

"What's that got to do with me?"

"Most of his men left in town are here in the saloon. I checked to be sure when I came in. I want them distracted so there's no chance of them noticing me leave with Elaine."

"You want me to keep their attention?" She was obviously already mulling over the idea.

"Yeah. Keep them occupied long enough for us to get clear of town. Can you handle it?"

She grinned cynically. "It's easy to get men like that interested. I'll keep them occupied, sure enough. It won't be the first time I've entertained a roomful of men." Hard, black shadows moved in her eyes. "Of course, this might call for something special," she added musingly.

"Don't put yourself in any danger," Clint advised.

"I've been in danger from men ever since I first put on a petticoat," she retorted bitterly. The evil shadows still lurked in her eyes. "Don't worry about me. Just see to it you get that little schoolgirl out of here before she gets hurt. Heaven knows, with the way I've seen Carter act about her, I've been tempted to scratch out her eyes myself!''

''Just keep the men occupied. I'll do the rest.''

She gave him a roguish smile. ''When do you want the show to start, cowboy?''

''Give me a half hour. I'll be ready to move by then. I'll leave here by the back door so that no one will see us together.''

''A half hour it is.'' She turned toward the door, then paused and glanced back over her shoulder. ''You know,'' she said almost wistfully, ''if it wasn't for this town, I could have been a lady too.''

''I reckon you could,'' Clint told her.

She looked quickly away from him. The lantern light shone like fire off her red hair. She snatched open the door and was gone. Clint heard her passage down the hallway.

He waited a few seconds longer, then headed out the rear of the saloon. He hadn't given himself much time. Quickly he moved through the darkness toward the stable.

He had seen no further sign of Ratter. No doubt the little man would be eager to tell Brandon at the first opportunity that Clint had been talking with Rhonda. By then, Clint prayed, it would be too late.

When will Clint come? Elaine asked herself. She knew he was coming. She had known since his loudly telling Sledger of Carter's imminent departure. Then, a little later, she had seen Carter ride out with his men. Surely it wouldn't be much longer.

Restlessly, she moved about the parlor. There had been little enough for her to do in preparation. They would have to travel light, she knew. And, actually, there were few of the fine things from Carter that she cared to take with her. The clothes and jewelry all seemed tainted now.

She had prepared some supplies and packed a small valise with her Bible and a few items of clothing. Next she had donned her riding outfit. Vieja was not in the house, which saddened her. She had closed the parlor window and drawn the drapes so that Sledger wouldn't hear her moving about or see her clad in her riding skirt.

How long had Carter been gone? she wondered. Maybe she had misunderstood. Perhaps Clint was not coming after all. She shivered with the deliciously re- membered intimacy of his arms enfolding her and his lips finding hers. No, she had not misunderstood. He would come.

She ran her hands lightly over the smooth ivory keys of the piano, but did not depress them. She would miss her piano, she reflected with sadness. Its music had given her comfort and solace over the long days and nights of her imprisonment here. And she had been a prisoner from the very beginning, she realized. She had simply been too blind to see it.

She left the parlor and strode to the kitchen at the

rear of the house. For a moment she peered out into the darkness. She could see nothing. She realized she was wringing her hands and forced herself to stop.

Impulsively she returned to the parlor. As she stepped out of the darkened hallway into the lighted room, a footfall sounded behind her and she turned sharply. Her breath caught in her throat.

Stocking cap in place, Sledger was leering down at her. He must have entered the house while she was in the kitchen, and have waited in the shadows of the hallway for her return. She backed slowly away from him.

He took a deliberate step in pursuit. "Well, you done talked to Brandon and he didn't come gunning for me," he said in his gravel voice. "Guess that means you took our little talk to heart, and you decided you wouldn't mind me paying you a nice, friendly visit now and again when he's gone." He advanced another step. He didn't seem to notice her riding attire. He had other things on his mind. She became aware that she was cornered. "Makes me mighty happy, you being so agreeable and all." He spread his lips and started toward her.

Elaine snatched a vase from the lamp table and hurled it at his grinning face.

His big hand arose with incredible speed to bat the vase aside. It shattered into fragments at the impact of his knuckles. His grin altered in a hideous fashion. "So you got some spunk left, after all. Just what I'd expect from a spirited little filly. Well, I'll just have to break you to halter."

As he prepared to lunge, Elaine caught a glimpse of movement from the hallway. There was a low growl like that of a mother puma protecting her young, and then Vieja flung herself out of the darkness at Sledger. A huge knife gleamed in her hand. Elaine gave a horrified scream.

Sledger was gone from the porch, Clint saw. He felt a quick knotting of dread. He tugged hard on the lead rope of the horses he led through the shadows. Then Elaine's scream split the night. Clint dropped the rope and sprinted. He went over the picket fence with a bound and sprang up onto the porch. He paused, but could hear nothing more. He bared gun and blade and went through the door. The lighted doorway to the parlor was ahead of him. He plunged down the hall and burst into the room.

"Sledger!" he roared.

Elaine was sprawled on the love seat where she had been knocked or shoved. Sledger stood like a colossus in the center of the parlor. A slight nick was on one arm. Gripped by throat and wrist, her kicking feet clear of the floor, Vieja writhed helplessly in his grip.

Clint had no target for a snap shot. He jerked the Colt up to aim, and Sledger hurled the old woman full at him. Clint couldn't avoid her, and she crashed into him, all flailing bony limbs and wiry body. He went down under the impact. His gun and knife flew from his fingers. Desperately, he thrust Vieja from atop him and scrambled onto his feet. He was in trouble, bad trouble. He'd let himself be disarmed like an amateur, and now there was nothing for it but to meet Sledger on his own bare-knuckle terms.

He was barely fast enough in regaining his feet. Sledger hadn't waited. Clint got a glimpse of his battered features behind a big right fist that sped at his skull like a cannonball. It was a killer blow. Sledger was trying to finish this fast. Clint hunched low and ducked aside from the punch. It scraped past his head and tore his Stetson loose. He felt as though his ear was gone too. He pumped his own right hand in low, and it connected with the concrete hardness of Sledger's body. Then Sledger's hooking left seemed to tear his jaw off its hinges. The blow spun him around and into the room.

Sledger was after him as if he were coming out of his corner at the start of a round. His fists were up, his big body poised and dangerous. But this wasn't a prizefight. There were no rules here and Sledger wasn't trying for a knockout. He was trying for a kill.

"All right, gunfighter," he rasped. "The fight just started." The minor wound apparently inflicted by Vieja wasn't slowing him.

Clint got his fists up, elbows in to protect his body. He was no novice at fighting without weapons, but he'd never made his living at it.

Sledger came in fast and confident. His fists battered Clint's blocking forearms back against his chest. Then his onrushing right fist filled Clint's vision. He bobbed his head, and the hard knuckles smashed into his forehead rather than between his eyes. He staggered back until his spine slammed painfully against the piano.

Immediately, Sledger attacked him with powerful slugging blows. He had his man on the ropes. Clint let his upper body fall back onto the solid surface of the piano for a brace. He yanked up his legs, pulled his knees to his chest, and shot both feet out. The soles of his driving boots caught Sledger in the lower face and upper chest, and he went reeling away, his bent arms working to regain his balance. As he collided with the bookcase, a shower of books rained down on him. Cursing, he pushed himself back into the fray.

Clint sidestepped clear of the piano and kicked the lamp table into Sledger's path. Barely looking, Sledger booted it into splinters. Clint had a glimpse of Elaine still sprawled dazedly on the love seat. Vieja lay motionless near the door. He had no time to see more. Sledger was almost close enough to bring his fists into play again.

But Sledger surprised him. Clint was watching his hands when the boxer threw a kick, low and hard. Clint twisted off balance to avoid it, and Sledger came around with a right hand that smashed into the side of his skull. Clint crashed back through the window and onto the porch, shattering glass as he went. The curtain protected him, but he still felt shards bite into his back and arms as he thrashed to untangle himself from its folds.

He made it up on his feet, head ringing. Sledger was framed in the window, just clambering through. Clint drove a right of his own to the square unguarded jaw. Sledger grunted, but his arms thrust him on and out of the window. Clint shot out his hands and caught Sledger's shirt. He threw himself backward off the porch. Sledger was yanked with him. In midair, Clint twisted his body, and when they hit the ground, Sledger was half beneath him.

Fingers like claws of iron came at his face and eyes. Clint flung himself rolling clear. Sledger surged up onto his feet. He charged with his head down like the bull buffalo that Clint had seen out on the prairie. It was another brawler's trick, but this time Clint wasn't caught by surprise. He pivoted out of Sledger's path and put all the force of his turn behind the right fist he threw at Sledger's ear. It sent Sledger's charge veering off to one side, where his heavy body collided with the picket fence. A section of it was flattened beneath him as he went down.

For a moment Clint was too winded to go after him. Dimly, he noted that there was a peculiar brightness to the night. A muffled roaring was in his ears. The air felt hot on his face.

Sledger clambered to his feet, the splintered remains of the fence falling from him. His stocking cap was askew, and he reached up to tug it straight. *Round two,* Clint thought dazedly. He felt as if he'd already been trampled by a wild bronc. Faintly he thought he heard shouts. Was the fight going to draw a crowd now that it was out in the open? He had to end it soon.

He went to meet Sledger, forcing his legs to steadiness. As he closed, he faked with his right hand and then tried a kick of his own, stabbing the toe of his boot at Sledger's knee. Sledger turned his leg like a dancer to avoid it, and then he whipped a wicked left in under Clint's rib cage. Clint twisted sideward under the blow. Sledger's right came at his jaw, and after that, for a few bruising moments, Clint lost track of the fists striking him.

He fetched up hard against the porch. This fight was going to end soon, all right. It was going to end with him dead. Sledger struck at him again. Clint let his legs sag. He dropped to his knees and lunged at the pillars of Sledger's legs. Briefly his arms encircled them. Then Sledger's knee jerked up to his jaw, and his head rocked back far enough to see the strangely lit sky overhead. He slumped sideways against the porch.

Sledger's black figure loomed hugely over him, one big fist drawn back past his head. As if it were a mallet, he swung it around and down at Clint's skull. Like a sledgehammer on stone, that blow would crack his skull, Clint realized. Desperately, he drove his open hands up to catch that descending arm. The force behind it buckled his arms back to his chest, but he stayed the blow. Before Sledger could jerk free, Clint wrapped his legs around one of Sledger's and then twisted hard with his lower body. Sledger crashed to the ground beside him.

Clint scrambled to get clear. Cruel hands caught him and pulled him back. Sledger lurched up onto his feet, hauling Clint erect with him. Again, Clint was pinned against the porch. Sledger's left hand gripped shirt and flesh to hold him steady. His clenched fist drew back past his ear.

Clint reached out with both hands and yanked the stocking cap down over Sledger's eyes. Sledger howled in rage. Instead of finishing his punch, he clawed at the blinding cap. Clint hit him right and left, braced himself more solidly against the porch, and did it again. Sledger's head rocked back and forth. Clint drove an uppercut to his jaw. Sledger's hands came up in a blind attempt to guard his head. Clint pistoned his elbows and slugged with both fists to his body.

Sledger doubled halfway over beneath the assault. He swung wildly, but there was no strength or coordination to the blows. Clint drove his fists at the stocking cap, and felt solid flesh beneath the woolen fabric.

Sledger groped for him in darkness. Clint fended the clawing hands aside. Triumph was a wild flame within him. He turned, wrapped his arms around Sledger's covered head, and wrestled him over double. Then he drove him headfirst into the porch with all the strength he could summon up through his legs and arms and chest. Boards splintered and cracked. An awful shudder ran through Sledger's body. His weight sagged against Clint's arms. Clint dropped him and staggered weakly back. Sledger didn't move.

"Fight's over," Clint rasped.

He was panting and dizzy. Only slowly did he become aware of shouting voices, the weird roar, and the flickering light he had vaguely noted during the fight. He turned round and bit back an exclamation of shock.

Flames licked up toward the night sky from the collection of saloons and dance halls lining the main street. Running figures were silhouetted against them. With dawning horror, Clint understood that Rhonda had given him his distraction. And she had taken the opportunity to wreak her vengeance on this and all the other honky-tonk towns she had known over the hard, mean years. She had set Beer City on fire.

Whether she had really intended it to get completely out of control, he didn't know. But the fire had found ready fuel in the tents and wooden structures of the town. As he watched, the flames leaped to a large tent and flared even higher. The fire was advancing. Soon, even Brandon's house might be in danger. A hot wind licked at his face.

Some frantic efforts were being made to fight the flames, he saw. He figured they wouldn't do a lot of good. And there was no way that he could be of much help. He put his back to the nightmare scene as Elaine and Vieja emerged from the house. They didn't appear to be seriously hurt, just shaken by their desperate struggle with Sledger. From the porch, they stared in awe at the flames.

"We've got to get moving!" Clint shouted. He looked about and saw the horses still tethered to one another. Thankfully, they hadn't bolted. "I've got a horse for Vieja too!"

He bounded up the steps, fighting to throw off the effects of the brutal brawl. "Brandon had a strongbox brought here," he said to Elaine. "Where is it?"

Her face was pale in the light of the approaching flames. She stared at him in confusion.

He went on: "Brandon stole that strongbox from one of the men I work for. And now Brandon's on his way to take him hostage and then kill him!"

"We must stop him!" she cried. "I think the strongbox is in the storeroom by the kitchen."

Inside, Clint retrieved his gun and knife and hat. He found the strongbox where Elaine had thought it would be. He lugged it out, grunting at its weight. Elaine had brought the horses to the picket fence by the time he emerged onto the porch. With great effort, he wrestled the box onto the spare horse he had brought for that purpose. He secured it quickly.

Elaine was talking in low, passionate tones to Vieja when he finished. "Please come with us, Vieja," she urged.

Vieja shook her head. "No more white man's ways for this one," she said. "I go back to my people." For a few seconds she looked at Clint with wise, solemn eyes. "He take care of you now," she told Elaine.

"I'll miss you, Vieja!" Elaine hugged her tightly. Reluctantly she drew back.

Vieja mounted with a feline agility that belied her age. Her horse pounded away into the night. Tears were on Elaine's face.

Clint looked toward the fire. Both sides of the street were burning now, and the flames were spreading down the narrow side roads. A riderless horse pounded past in panic-stricken flight. Flaming debris flew overhead.

Suddenly, from the far end of town, a brighter light flared briefly into existence and backlighted the burning buildings. Then the dull rumble of an explosion rolled through the heated air. Somehow, Clint realized, the flames had reached the still on Hog Creek. White City was dying in a fiery agony.

He became conscious of Elaine's fingers gripping his arm. The horses were beginning to stir restlessly. "Let's ride!" he yelled.

She nodded and moved woodenly to her horse. As she clambered into the saddle, Clint swung astride his paint. The horses needed no urging, and they fled the heated roar of the flames. Clint remembered Vieja's final statement, and he hoped fervently that he would live long enough to make her prediction come true.

He glanced back once as they rode. The inferno lit the night sky behind them.

Chapter Eleven

T hom Chancery felt the slowing of the train, and sat up on the couch in the Pullman. He had spent the night there, dozing fitfully, nagged by a growing uneasiness. He had overlooked something important, he thought. He had made some mistake that could prove costly.

Herns had retired to the bedroom and Geoffrey to the tiny servant's quarters. Chancery had remained restlessly awake until at last, fully clothed except for his suit coat, he had forced himself to stretch out on the couch.

Now he pushed himself to his feet. What was happening? Why was the train slowing? The sunlight shining through the windows showed it to be early morning. His joints ached and his mouth was fuzzy. He blinked painfully against the sunshine as he peered out the window. He could see nothing to alarm him on the rolling grassland.

A respectful knocking at the Pullman's front door made him straighten. One of the two crewmen must have come back to advise them of what was causing the train to slow. Just the same, he touched the butt of the the snub-nosed revolver in his shoulder holster as he moved down the car to the door.

Mac, the assistant engineer, bobbed his head in greeting when he opened the door to the small iron platform outside the Pullman's front end. The wind of their passage blew across Chancery's face and the roar of the locomotive grew louder.

"What is it?" He raised his voice to be heard.

Mac was frowning. "We're not sure, Mr. Chancery. There's some kind of barrier with three or four horsemen up the track. Jake's slowing down some, but he didn't want to stop without your say-so."

Chancery scowled, trying to make his thoughts orderly. "How far outside of Liberal are we?"

"A long ways yet. There ain't nothing nearby right now except grass."

Alarm bells were ringing in Chancery's mind. He turned sharply away from the doorway and pulled back the curtains to peer out the window on the opposite side of the car. In a moment he saw what he was afraid he'd see. The figures of at least a half-dozen horsemen were just cresting a hill a hundred yards away. As he watched, they came racing down toward the slowing train. He didn't need to see more.

He jerked himself back to the door. "Keep this rig moving!" he shouted. "Open the throttle and flatten that barricade! Don't stop for anything! We're coming under attack!"

Mac gave a startled acknowledgment and disappeared. Chancery snatched out his pistol and checked the loads as he moved toward the door to Herns's bedroom. He cursed himself as a fool for overlooking what now seemed obvious. He had taken extra precautions to protect the millionaire's holdings, but he had never anticipated an attack on Herns himself. It had been too long since he'd played a bodyguard's role, he told himself bitterly.

Herns himself emerged before he could knock to summon him. "What's going on, Thom?" The millionaire was still in his nightclothes.

"Some riders are coming after the train, Mr. Herns," Chancery explained. "I don't like the looks of it. There's also a barricade on the tracks ahead. I've instructed the engineer not to stop."

He could feel the train picking up speed even as he spoke. Mac had moved with alacrity to convey his orders. Herns brushed past him to gaze out the window. He didn't appear to be losing his head in the crisis, Chancery noted with approval.

"May I be of assistance, gentlemen?" Geoffrey had appeared from his quarters. He was unshaven but fully dressed.

"Take down those rifles and get them loaded!" Chancery snapped. "I expect we'll be needing them."

A bullet exploded through glass and lodged in the car's fine wooden paneling. All three men ducked instinctively. Geoffrey sprang toward the mounted hunting rifles. Chancery knelt on the narrow divan attached beneath the windows. He tugged the window open and felt the slipstream whip at his face. Outside the train, he could see the riders racing parallel to it, six-guns spitting fire.

Another bullet smashed glass. "By the heavens, hand me one of those rifles!" Herns exclaimed.

Chancery thrust his revolver out the window and triggered off at a rider racing alongside. The wind snatched the sound of the shot away. A miss. The short-barreled pistol wasn't meant for this type of running gun battle. The train's whistle sounded. Jake was giving warning to the riders at the barricade.

Chancery sensed rather than heard a shattering impact from the front of the train. A moment later fragments of splintered wood went flying past the car. The cowcatcher on the locomotive had smashed the barricade, he realized with satisfaction.

But they weren't out of danger. The riders still bade fair to stop the train, which hadn't yet picked up enough speed to outrun their horses. One daring bandit swung in close like a trick rider and flung himself at the tender car behind the engine. Chancery twisted and tried a shot at his nimble figure. But the fellow vanished agilely from view. He had managed to board the train.

More bullets were striking the car. Chancery fired again, then risked a glance over his shoulder. Geoffrey had just positioned himself at the opposite window with one of the rifles. He seemed to know what he was doing with it.

At least a dozen riders were flanking the train. Herns put one knee on the divan next to him and used the barrel of his big hunting rifle to smash the rest of the glass from a shattered window. He snugged the butt against his shoulder, led one of the riders for a pair of seconds, then fired. The report of the big weapon was deafening. Herns cursed softly as his target raced on, unhit. Geoffrey's rifle exploded from the other side of the car. Chancery couldn't see if the shot was effective.

Herns broke his rifle to reload. One of the riders veered in close to the car. Chancery thrust his Colt at him and fired almost point-blank. The man seemed to be snatched off his horse. Chancery glimpsed him rolling to a halt beside the track behind them.

Herns's rifle went off again. This time a rider was hurled sideward from his mount beneath the impact of the big slug. Herns cried out in triumph and jacked the rifle open to reload.

"They've gotten aboard, sir!" Geoffrey shouted. "At least two of them!"

Chancery felt his heart sinking. Mac and Jake were unarmed up in the cab of the engine. With the attackers aboard the train now, and others still racing alongside, it was only a matter of time before they would be at their mercy. At that instant he glimpsed the face of yet another rider reining in close to the Pullman. With a shock of horrified recognition, everything became all too clear. "Brandon!" he gasped. They didn't stand a chance.

* * *

"We need to rest the horses," Clint told Elaine. He wasn't sure how far they were from the rail line, but they had been pushing the animals hard.

They dismounted and he loosened the cinches on his horse and the packhorse. He turned to help Elaine, but saw with approval that she had already tended to her animal. In the dim predawn light he watched her fuss over the horse.

Then she looked around and caught his gaze. There had been little chance for conversation during their ride. "Who do you work for?" she asked. He couldn't make out the expression on her face.

Briefly he told her about the Partners and the varied tasks he performed for them.

"I knew you weren't a gunfighter," she said when he had finished.

Clint shrugged. "Still a hired gun."

She took a small step toward him. "Why haven't you ever quit?"

"I guess I never found a reason."

She looked down. "And now?" came her quiet voice.

"The Good Book says there's a time to kill and a time to heal," he said hoarsely. "I've been killing for an awful long time."

She raised her eyes to his face. "Does that mean you've found a reason to stop?"

Clint reached her in a stride. She came willingly into

his arms. "You're my reason," he said into the soft, dark warmth of her hair. "I love you."

"Thank God, Clint. I love you too."

Clint stiffened. "Listen!" he said. From far off came the wail of a train's whistle. He swung his head in that direction.

The killing couldn't stop just yet.

As they topped the hill, Clint could see the train on the plain below. It wasn't moving at top speed although it was accelerating. Smoke and cinders belched from its smokestack. Riders raced beside it. He could see the tiny flames of their handguns, and even over the noise of the train, he heard the faint pop of gunshots too. Return fire was coming from the single passenger car. There was no caboose. From this distance he couldn't pick out Brandon, but he spotted at least two figures clambering about on the cars.

The attack was underway, but the outcome was still undecided. Their grueling ride had not been in vain.

The locomotive wasn't yet even with their position. He slid his Winchester from its sheath and asked Elaine, "Can you use this?"

Her face was drawn with weariness, but she managed a spirited nod.

He didn't question how she had come by the ability. They were heavily outnumbered and every gun would count. He handed her the rifle and nodded at the desperate race below. "Throw some lead at the riders," he ordered. "I'm going down there."

"Be careful." She took the rifle.

Clint didn't wait. He put heels to the paint and sent him down the slope. Behind him he heard the first crack of the Winchester. As he came out on the flats, his exhaustion fell away from him. The train and riders were passing in front fifty yards ahead. He glimpsed a lone rider swing himself from his saddle to the rear of the Pullman. Something in his daredevil horsemanship was familiar.

He angled the paint at a run to intercept the train. Another shot sounded from the hill at his back. A rider flung up his arms and tumbled from his horse. Elaine hadn't lied; she could use the rifle with deadly skill. Clint had no clear count of the enemy, but one of their number was down.

He was closing fast on another attacker. He pulled his six-gun. Applications of bacon grease while on the ride from White City had eased the swelling from his fight with Sledger. The butt of the Colt fit snugly in his fist.

The rider saw him coming. Clint recognized him as one of Brandon's enforcers. The gunman must have read his hostile intent. He twisted about in the saddle to bring his revolver to bear as Clint bore down on him. Clint thrust the Colt out, thumbed back the hammer, and fired. He fired again as flame stabbed at him from the enforcer's gun. One or both of his shots drove the gunman reeling back in his saddle. He slid from it, a boot catching in his stirrup as he fell. Clint lost sight of his flailing figure dragged behind the panicked horse.

For the moment no other attackers were in view. Clint put the paint to running even with the Pullman. The train was moving at a good clip now and the paint was tired. He hoped the animal was up to what he was asking of him. He heeled the horse to greater speed. For long seconds they matched the train as it roared across the prairie. Then, slowly, the paint began to gain.

Clint edged him closer. The thunder of the engine was deafening. Black and monstrous, it loomed huge beside him, dwarfing him and the horse with its bulk. The iron wheels were almost as tall as the withers of the paint.

He drew even with the cab of the engine. Open to the air, a big, square portal was set in the side of the engineer's compartment. Wind-whipped smoke lashed Clint's eyes, and for an instant the figures within the compartment blurred before his vision. When his eyes cleared, he saw a gunman framed in the portal, gripping the rim with his left hand for balance as he threw down with the revolver in his right.

Clint snapped up his own six-shooter and fired. The barrel was just five feet from his target and it was lined dead center. The enforcer plunged headfirst from the engineer's compartment, and his rolling body was swept away by the train's passage.

Clint glimpsed at least one more attacker in the crowded compartment, and he was locked in a struggle with two crewmen. Unable to place a clear shot, Clint shoved the .45 back in his holster and cast his eyes up at the black mass of the locomotive in front of the cab. There was no place to grab there. The pumping rods would chew him to shreds.

He eased up lightly on the paint and let the tender car behind the locomotive pull even with him. Carefully he laid the reins against the paint's sweating neck and worked him in close. He had a distorted view of the animal's wild, rolling eye. Then the side of the car was within arm's reach. One slip now and he would go down beneath the churning wheels.

He shot out a straining hand and clamped it around the horizontal grab-iron at the rear corner of the car. Without even time for a prayer, he kicked free of the stirrups and let the train's passage yank him from the saddle.

He felt the awful jerk as his shoulder was all but torn from its socket. For a horrifying second it felt as though his body were snapped out full length alongside the train. Then his other hand caught the grab-iron and he was scrambling with his feet to gain purchase. He got his toes wedged between the grab-iron and the car, and hung there for an eternity of an instant.

A short metal ladder was mounted to the rear of the car. He twisted his body about until he could reach out for it with clawing fingers. The steel tracks were rushing past beneath him. He could feel the seemingly limitless power of the iron horse to which he clung, and smell the acrid, oily scent of its smoke.

He caught the ladder and hauled himself over to it with an effort that cracked his joints. He was aboard the train with an uncertain number of Brandon's gun hawks—and maybe even Brandon himself. Herns and Chancery were almost certainly in danger at this very moment, but restoring control of the locomotive to friendly hands had to be the first order of business.

He straightened his legs and started up the ladder. He looked up just as his head came past the edge of the car's roof, and found himself staring down the barrel of a leveled six-gun with a fierce mustached face behind it. He had no idea where the man had come from—and no time to ponder it. Death was inches away.

He snaked up a desperate hand and caught the thick wrist behind the gun. In one motion he twisted the wrist and yanked back and down, swinging his upper body out and away from the ladder. With a startled scream, the gunman hurtled past him. His voice was chopped off as suddenly as if by an ax. Clint didn't look down.

Next he heaved himself up onto the catwalk atop the tender car. Briefly he crouched there. A single rider was off wide to his right. He pulled his Colt and aimed a shot at him. The fellow veered his horse away and let the train outdistance him.

Clint straightened to a crouch and catfooted forward the length of the car. Balance was tricky on the swaying surface. At the front of the car, just behind the engine, he dropped flat on his belly. Gun in fist, he inched forward and peered down into the open rear of the engineer's compartment.

One of the crewmen lay sprawled with a bloody chest on the floor of the small cab. His partner was slowing the train, the barrel of the enforcer's revolver in his back.

As if sensing Clint's gaze, the enforcer glanced back and up over his shoulder. His eyes widened and he started to turn. Clint shot him between the shoulder blades. The engineer gaped up at Clint as the gunman crumpled at his feet.

"Open the throttle!" Clint shouted down to him. "Keep her highballing!" They couldn't afford to slow or stop the train until the threat of danger was past.

The engineer gave a stunned nod in response. Clint wriggled backward until his head was no longer over the gap between the cars. Somewhere in his wild storming of the train he had lost his hat, he realized. He reloaded his Colt by feel while he scanned the surrounding countryside. He spotted only a couple of riders shrinking away in the distance. They, at least, had given up the fight.

Where was Brandon? As long as he remained unaccounted for, Clint couldn't consider the danger to be over. He recalled the familiar rider he had seen leap onto the rear of the train. A bleak certainty grew in him. Brandon was aboard the train; he was in the Pullman with his prey.

Clint moved to the end of the tender where he could peer cautiously at the solid front door of the private car. Another door was at the rear of such conveyances, he knew. That was how Brandon would have gained entrance. There were no grab-irons or railings along the sides of the car, and so there was no way to get a look inside through the windows. There was also no way to guess whether Brandon would be expecting an assault from the front or the back. Clint didn't like it. He would have to bulldog this one head-on.

Carefully he eased down the ladder and stepped across to the small metal platform in front of the door. The thunder of the engine drowned any sounds that might have come from within. He couldn't count on surprise. Brandon would have felt the train picking up speed. And he may well have seen the bodies of his men falling by the tracks. He would know a dangerous enemy was aboard.

Clint gripped his Colt. He braced himself against the platform railing and lifted a booted foot. In a single movement he smashed the sole against the lock on the door and burst through as it swung open.

He had a fragmented impression of a long, narrow living area that ran much of the length of the coach. Thom Chancery was sprawled across a low divan with a hand pressed to his bloody side. Herns and a slighter, gray-haired man were crouched at the rear of the car. In front of them, as if he had, in fact, been waiting, was Carter Brandon. The Bergmann pistol in his fist was leveled at Clint's chest.

Clint fired with the reflex of all the long years spent living by the pull of a trigger. A fraction of a second later, the blast of the Bergmann merged with the roar of the Colt. Brandon jerked back and then sideways. Clint shot again, because he couldn't risk any chances with the man or his rapid-firing pistol. He didn't know where Brandon's single bullet had gone.

The gun boss collapsed across a reading seat. The Bergmann clattered to the floor. Clint ran forward and kicked the pistol far away.

Brandon stared at him from dimming eyes. "Bradlock," he gasped. "I saw you coming. What are you doing? Why'd you turn on me?"

"I took your place with the Partners," Clint told him.

Brandon managed a mirthless snort. "I should have known better than to trust a man so much like me."

"Not like you," Clint said. *Not ever,* he added to himself.

Suddenly Brandon shuddered. "You beat me," he said faintly. "Even with the Bergmann, you beat me."

"I told you," Clint murmured. "It depends on the man."

Brandon shuddered again. His wide-set eyes went glassy just before they closed for good.

Clint dropped the Colt back into his holster. Herns and the gray-haired man were just picking themselves up from the floor.

"Glad you could make it, Clint," Chancery rasped from between teeth gritted in pain. "He got the drop on me."

"You weren't the first," Clint told him.

"There's still one rider coming after us." The gray-haired man had moved to peer out the window like an old soldier checking the field of battle. He gave a startled exclamation. "Well, I'll be! It looks like a young woman, and a pretty one at that! She appears to be leading a horse that's carrying a strongbox!"

Clint's legs suddenly wobbled beneath him. He sat down on the low divan beside the window and grinned at Herns. "She has your gold, sir," he said. "Let's stop this train so that she can catch up."

"The reports are that White City burned to the ground," Chancery told Clint. "There's nothing much left of it but ashes—and good riddance. All the people there managed to get clear of the fire." He shifted his weight stiffly in his chair. His bandaged wound still pained him. He gazed at the other two people seated with him in the lavish hotel suite. "There was no sign of an old Indian woman or a red-haired saloon girl such as you described."

"Vieja's back with her people, then," Clint mused aloud. He hoped that Rhonda would manage to find a place to start over and become a lady.

"How is Mr. Herns?" Elaine asked solicitously. She looked prim and proper and very fetching in the lacy white dress that was part of the wardrobe that Herns had insisted on rewarding her with. A white ribbon was set in her black hair.

"He's headed back East," Chancery informed her,

"and just a little the worse for wear. He had a board meeting to attend in Chicago."

"What about you?"

"I'll be all right. Brandon didn't have time to do much more than plug me and then cover Mr. Herns and Geoffrey before Clint showed up. I can't say I'm sorry to see Mr. Herns go. I'll take managing the Partners' business assets out here anytime over playing nursemaid to one of them! Still, I've got to admit he held his own when the shooting started. Oh, and incidentally," he added, "Mr. Herns did say the hotel rooms are yours for as long as you want to stay here in Liberal. He'll foot the bill."

"Elaine and I do have a little bit of business to tend to before we head back to Guthrie," Clint said casually. "As soon as we're done with you, we're fixing to look up a preacher and see about having us a wedding."

Chancery looked back and forth between them. "I've seen the way you two look at each other," he said. "Getting married probably isn't a bad idea." He grinned at Elaine's sudden blush and downcast eyes.

"I'll be needing a best man," Clint told him.

"Well, you've got him, even if he is a bit shot up!" Chancery assured him heartily. "And Mr. Herns wanted me to tell you one other thing, Clint. There was talk of a bonus for this job back in Guthrie. In addition to cash, the Partners are going to have a full section of prime land in the Territory conveyed into your name."

"Do you figure they could make that a wedding present and put it in both our names?" Clint drawled.

"I'm sure they could." Chancery eyed Clint soberly. "Does this mean I'm going to have to find a replacement for you on their payroll?"

Clint recalled the silent vow he had made to himself back on the Pullman and the promise he had given Elaine. There would be no more lost souls to haunt his conscience, no more young kids with guns on dusty streets. "I reckon it does," he replied firmly. "A man can't settle down to ranching and raising a family if he always has to ride herd on other men's property."

Then his eyes turned to Elaine. The Good Book said that a virtuous woman was worth far more than rubies. His time for healing had begun.